Calling for Snow

HEATHER MCPEAKE

1.

ALL I WANT FOR CHRISTMAS is for my ex to stop looking at me across this bar like I might take him home. I want this more than I wanted the Easy Bake Oven I begged for when I was ten, the opal engagement ring I'd been hoping for last year, and a refill on the fizzy cocktail sitting on the bar in front of me, which I've drained down to the twist of lemon peel. I know I'm too old to believe in Santa, but I'm also too young to have given up on love and a little too lonely to trust myself to make good decisions. The warm glow of these string lights and the fact that there isn't a genie hiding at the bottom of that bottle of gin tells me everything I need to know.

I need a chaperone.

The problem is that Matilda's is emptier than usual at eight o'clock on a Thursday night. Maybe I could thank the marathon of ugly sweater parties, obligatory holiday travel plans, or Holly Danford at News Channel 10, who has been swearing through her million-watt smile that there's snow in the forecast. Half of everywhere closed early because of it, even though the streets and sidewalks have been salted like the rim of a margarita and it hasn't snowed, in any way that could be considered more than a powdered-sugar-on-your-French-toast kind of dusting, in the entire ten-plus years I've lived here.

Regardless of the reason, I have a relatively unobstructed view of him sitting at a booth along the wall. I wonder if that's the one where our names are squeezed in among hundreds of others, written in a bright shade of Sharpie that turned out to be more permanent than our relationship: Nate + Cecilia. I'd actually used a plus sign, like the two of us were some sort of mathematical equation. As if the wanna-be celebrity chef and the semi-professional wedding photographer would equal that forever kind of love.

You should know I've always been bad at math.

He's wearing short sleeves even though it's twenty degrees outside. I don't have to glance over again to know that it's probably to show off the tattoo sleeve that has spread further down his arm at some point over the past four months. He's sitting with friends I recognize but don't know, which is a small mercy. They all seem to be home for the holidays, just like him. The vibe tonight is a little too Ghosts of Christmas Past for me, but it's too cold to justify the short walk home.

The problem is that I actually might take him home, especially if I have another drink and start feeling sorry for myself, the way I have been ever since I spent Thanksgiving eating takeout Chinese in my pajamas and watching *Love Actually* on repeat. The longer I sit here watching him toss me sidelong smiles and looking like a long lost Hemsworth, the more I wonder why we ever broke up, even though I know perfectly well the answer to that. Everybody knows the answer to that: my mom, my therapist, my friends. It was so unbelievable to me that I'd been repeating it like a mantra for the past few months, as if playing it on repeat might finally make it make sense to me.

"I'm not ready to settle down."

The thing is, I thought we had been talking about the very opposite of settling down when he said this. Somewhere between serving me a bowl of shrimp and grits and asking if it could use more gouda, he tells me that he's had an epiphany.

"I want to start a food truck."

Being the supportive girlfriend I was, I remember smiling. "Yeah? That's awesome. I think you should."

"In California."

"California?" I'd laughed. "What's in California?"

"Me," he said. "Next week."

"This is... what?" I said. "You're serious? We're just going to pick up and move to California?"

I still feel the sting of stupidity thinking about the excitement that had crept into my voice when I believed that *we* were moving to California instead of *he*. In that split second, my mind had already filled with images of the two of us road tripping across the country and unpacking our life into a mid-century modern ranch with tech savvy neighbors and an avocado tree in the backyard. I could see our summer wedding, with him in a gray suit and me in a simple ivory dress that swept straight to the floor, set against the backdrop of a candlelit vineyard that had been passed down through a tight-knit family of winemakers for three or four generations.

Not that any of those things were ridiculous assumptions, necessarily. We'd been together for two-and-a-half years. Not just together, but inseparable. He moved into my place after six months, with his ratty futon and more high-end cookware than we could comfortably fit in my kitchen, and he'd kissed my forehead and said it felt like fate. Just like all his ambitious reduction sauces and completely unnecessary aiolis, I'd eaten it right up. Everybody assumed we'd get married. Until we didn't. Now he's back, on my side of the Mississippi River, sitting in my neighborhood bar, looking at me like he's got a chance.

"Isn't that that guy you used to date?" a voice says.

I know who it belongs to even before he slides in beside me, wearing a sweater that reminds me of my grandpa and a self-satisfied smirk.

"Aren't you that asshole who lives next door to me?" I reply.

"Me? No. You must have me confused with someone else," he says. "I'm a delight."

I give him a flat, unamused gaze. "Right."

He flags down tonight's barkeep, Ari, who is always sweet to him even though I'm pretty sure she was once one of his infamous one-night-stands. I wonder if I've heard her scream his name through the too-thin wall that separates my living space from his. *Miles. Miles. Miles.* She wasn't the first and probably won't be the last, much to my dismay.

"Hey, honey," she says. "The usual?"

He gives her a nod, and she swipes my empty glass, asking if I want another. I think about my furnace that's barely working, the fact that the only thing waiting for me at home is a collection of engagement photos I haven't edited yet, and how Ari always floats the lemon twist just right so my drink looks like it belongs in a magazine. I sigh inwardly before nodding.

"You staying for the show?" Miles asks me.

When he tosses his head towards the piano near the front window, some of his summer-streaked hair goes with it. It's darkening with the seasons, the way it always does, like he's following the trend of every sorority girl who frequents this place when classes are in session. I'm always grateful to have it back when semester breaks send them home. I wish he would go home. The guitarist is setting up, and I know it's only a matter of time before The Devils & the Details takes the makeshift stage and regales us with all those kitschy songs we're beyond sick of hearing at this point in the season.

"Not on purpose," I say.

"That's the Christmas spirit."

The bell chimes as a few other twenty-somethings in scarves and hats filter in. They bring with them a woosh of cold, and I wrap myself more tightly in my cardigan. I'm acutely aware, with Miles standing next to me, that it's black, along with my skirt, boots, leggings, and, as he has too often been known to add, my soul. I can almost hear him thinking it as he gives me a once over, and I want to point out to him that my shirt is actually burgundy and that I came here straight from an early evening shoot: one of those cliche things that left me freezing in the bushes near a sparkling winter fountain while a guy proposed. Fairy lights twinkled in the background. There was a horse-drawn carriage waiting. She said yes, in case you were wondering.

If I'd known Nate was going to be here, I might have gone home and changed first. Not that he matters. He *doesn't* matter.

Ari slides Miles his Old Fashioned, and he lifts it to her with a nod before sauntering off towards the piano. A few moments later, his familiar chords fill the room. It's that same easy melody that keeps me up some nights, something he runs through to warm-up or when he's trying to annoy the fuck out of me at three a.m. I hate to admit it's pretty. I've caught it on loop in my head before, wondering only after the fact where it came from, like maybe I dreamed it. That's Miles for you. Filling women's heads with a song so they can't see what he really is.

Nate and I had watched enough of his conquests traipse to their cars in last night's clothes that we dubbed the shared front path between our door and his The Walk of Shame. Okay, maybe that isn't fair. He dated Nina, the brunette who always parked her Hummer right in front of my mailbox, for almost six months. He'd also stuck with Blair, the neonatal nurse who played Kings of Leon loud and on repeat, for about three, which was longer than I could stand listening to the one good song on that album over and over, so I have to give him credit on that one. The waitress with a hoop in her nose that worked at the fancy cocktail bar down the street, whose name I never got, lasted for about a month. Maybe there have been a few others, but they all seem to fade into the rotating blur of sighs and moans and a banging noise that sounded like they were doing actual construction on the other side of my bedroom wall, which I have to assume is also his bedroom wall. Lately, when I hear it, I just feel pathetic for being the one who ended up alone.

"Think it's really gonna snow?" Ari asks me, eyeing the frosty windows.

"Not a chance," I say. "You know it never snows here."

"Hey, a girl can hope, right?"

I can feel Nate watching me across the room, a suspicion I confirm with a single glance. As if he was waiting for this very thing, he smiles and returns his attention to the conversation, which includes a pixie-haired waif that just might be his backup if this thing with me falls through. The thought occurs to me, though, that maybe *I'm* the backup. Oh god.

I glance around the bar, which boasts only slightly more patrons than the last time I took inventory, and review my options. The guitarist in Miles's band looks like he recently emerged from twenty-five years living alone in the mountains, and his drummer is a skinny kid just out of college, who has hair bigger than he is and a Nietzche is My Homeboy sticker on the back window of his hatchback. So, those are a hard no. I also don't want to put forth the effort it would take to infiltrate any of the small groups that have filled up the tables near the front, and I doubt the couple having dinner at the other side of the bar needs a third.

I tap the screen of my phone, wondering what I am hoping to find there. I know there isn't anyone tonight I can call to my rescue. My best friend is in Chicago with her family. My parents have taken up temporary residence with my younger sister, who is a few days overdue with her first kid and subsequently doing nothing but fielding constant calls from her in-laws and walking on the treadmill until the baby comes out. And I'm sitting here. Alone.

It occurs to me that maybe it's not about what I want for Christmas, maybe it's about what I need. And what I need is for someone who didn't unceremoniously break my heart a few months ago to look at me like I might take him home, because it seems likely I'm taking *someone* home, and it absolutely can't be him. I might also need another drink. Definitely another drink.

***

Another thing you should know about me: I've never really had a one-night stand. I've done stay-up-all-night-sharing-your-soul marathons. I've made-out in hallways and backseats and even a few beds before thinking better of it. I've slept with some guys I liked but didn't love and even some I regretted later. But I've never had a one-night stand in the traditional sense of the term. Why do they call it that, anyway? Isn't the whole point to be somewhat horizontal? Maybe the fact that I don't know the answer to this is why my phone buzzes within twenty minutes of setting my masterplan in motion.

"Why are you on Spark?" Joss asks.

I plug one of my ears so I can hear her over the too bright chorus of "Winter Wonderland", where Miles is falling somewhere between indie rock frontman and classic crooner.

"You're in Chicago," I say. "How could you possibly know that I..."

The bar is slowly filling up around me, and I glance to either side, not wanting to advertise that I've just downloaded our generation's most notorious hookup app. Joss doesn't miss a beat.

"Because my grandmother has us out in the freezing ass cold, caroling, like we're in a fucking Dickens novel, and I'm bored out of my mind."

"And that makes you clairvoyant?"

"My account is set to your zip code," she laughs. "And unless you're trying to pick up chicks, you should switch your settings."

"Nobody says chicks anymore."

"Wait, *are* you trying to pick up chicks?"

"No."

"Then what the hell are you doing?" she chortles.

"The same thing everyone else is doing."

"Oh-kay," she says, like she doesn't at all believe me. "Well, this is good!"

"It is good," I agree. Then, "Why is it good?"

"Because you're putting yourself out there."

"Yup. That's me. All the way out there."

"And you've picked a helluva night. It's basically the trifecta. People are home for the holidays, already looking to get away from their families, and isn't it supposed to snow?"

"It's not going to snow."

I say it vehemently enough that the girl on the next stool shoots me a look before moving two seats down. I roll my eyes.

"My point is a lot of people are bored," Joss explains, "and it's a truth commonly acknowledged among singles everywhere that bored people are highly motivated to hookup."

"Lucky me," I say.

Applause rises around me. When I glance up again, I notice that a very viable-looking prospect has just eased up to the bar. He doesn't yet understand Ari's system, in which she serves all regulars before attending to new faces, regardless of who walked up first, but he's still wearing a half-smile and a puffy vest that makes him look young despite the beard. I smile, and the other half of his mouth lifts.

"Are you sure you're ready for this?" Joss asks.

"You know what they say," I offer. "Ready or not."

Bearded Vest Guy is still smiling. Normally I don't trust beards. They're kind of the oversized sunglasses of the guy world; you can't really be sure what someone looks like underneath them. Of course, that matters a lot less when you know you aren't going to stick around long enough for someone to shave his face.

"Well," she says, "when you know you know. Keep me updated. And prepare yourself for dick pics."

"Bye," I insist.

I realize I don't have the first fucking clue how to do this. I don't need a spark; I need an instant match-light, highly combustible, keep-away-from-open-flame situation. Something foolproof. Not that I'm a fool. No, it's actually worse: I'm a planner. I want a real-life romance, as silly as it sounds. I want a family, as dysfunctional as they can be. I want someone to share my life with, even if he drives me crazy some of the time. My plan has never included quick burnout passion, because it never seemed like something that was going to further any of these objectives. My plan also didn't include half of the shit that happened this past year, though, yet here I am. Adapt and overcome, right?

The band transitions to "All I Want for Christmas Is You". It's more My Chemical Romance than Mariah, and for some reason it fills me with tenuous courage. If Nate can show up in this bar – my bar – without a care in the world, then I can do the same. With a single lift of my glass, Ari appears in front of me.

"Hey, sweetie. What are you having?"

I toss my attention to Bearded Vest Guy.

"Whatever he's having," I say.

She follows my gaze across the bar and back, shrugging an eyebrow.

"You got it," she grins.

He's sitting next to me before the band gets to the line in the song about how they won't even wish for snow. They play it up appropriately, and the whoops and laughter of the thin crowd make the place feel full. It's hopeless trying to talk over the noise, so I just pass him a pint glass. His eyes are playful as he clicks it against my magazine cocktail before tipping it to his smile. And so, it begins.

2.

I MET NATE AT A WEDDING. I wish I was kidding. Maybe if I'd met him at the farmer's market, or in line at a pharmacy, or in a cramped auto-shop waiting room beside a scorched pot of coffee while getting my oil changed, the whole thing would've felt less romantic.

It wasn't the first wedding I'd shot, but it was definitely the biggest. I'd enlisted two assistants to help me with the event, and within the first fifteen minutes I realized it wasn't going to be enough. Four priests and a bishop had shown up to officiate the ceremony, and the wedding party included twelve groomsmen, who'd been intermittently passing around a flask of blackberry whiskey all afternoon, twelve bridesmaids, who'd been standing way too long in heels that day, and three flower girls under the age of five, one of whom was determined to show everyone she came in contact with her pink unicorn panties. They had so many guests they were fighting the fire department over seating, and the bride had a list a mile long of must-have shots. She wanted poses, she wanted candids, she basically wanted to be able to make a flipbook of the entire day, but with the polished, glossy radiance of a bridal catalog. We were run ragged before the ceremony even started.

Oh, and it rained. I'm not talking about a light drizzle, either. It was a gusty spring storm that tore blooms from the trees and left a cascade of water pouring off the top of the big white circus tent they'd set up for the outdoor reception, "in case of bad weather". The flapping side panels did very little to keep out the dampness. By the time the couple had finished their first dance, my hair was a wet mess twisted on top of my head, my mascara was a racoon smudge beneath my lash line, and my shoes made a squishing sound every time I took a step. Even with the waterproof precautions, I wondered if my camera equipment was going to survive the event. Hell, I wondered if I was going to survive the event.

It was eight o'clock. We still had three hours before the sparkler send-off, and I was sitting on one of the coolers the caterers had brought, crouched low behind a stack of drinkware crates, and questioning all of my life decisions. Maybe I should've listened to all those people who told me to get a "real" degree, like nursing or sales or anything that couldn't be considered a hobby.

But let's be honest, no one would do *this* for fun. Sunset mini sessions, seasonal family portraits, and intimate backyard weddings were usually fun. This was a disaster. It was also going to bring in enough money to cover my rent for the entire first month at the bungalow apartment I'd lucked into when I spotted the leaflet ad on the corkboard at Matilda's a few weeks earlier. I could afford to stay, but only if I kept up the big-ticket gigs like this. I'd thought I was ready. Now I was considering a failure-induced panic attack, when a guy with a vintage undercut and a black apron swooped around to retrieve a fresh tray of wine glasses.

"Hi," he said.

My eyes went wide, and for a moment I couldn't speak. His

stare slid over my features the way you might inspect a stray cat sitting on your porch. God, this was awkward. He looked like he might be ready to call for backup when his gaze landed on the camera.

"You're, uh... the photographer?"

"Yeah."

"Damn. I'm sorry," he said. To my confused look, he added, "I mean, this is kind of a shit show, am I right?"

Hearing someone else say it out loud felt hopeful. I loosened the clasp of my arms around my knees and was considering a response when he said, "You need a drink?"

I swelled with a breath.

"I don't think I really know what I need at this point. A time machine. A cloak of invisibility. A priest."

"That's some list," he offered. "Why a priest?"

"Last rites."

He laughed. "Well, I can't help you with the rest of it, but there's half a dozen members of the clergy at the table in the corner. I could give you a tray of salmon puffs, get you an easy in."

I smiled in spite of myself.

"No, thanks."

"I'm Nate."

"Cecilia."

He nodded in a way that made me want to wipe my eyes and straighten my hair. I kept my knees tucked into my chest, unwilling or perhaps unable to move, but my smile lingered.

"I've gotta get back to it," he said, "but feel free to hide out back here for as long as you like. You've got at least an hour before we take all your cover."

"I should probably get back out there, too," I admitted. "Is there a woman in a white dress glancing around frantically yet?"

"Not yet," he said, after a quick scan. "But the wedding

planner is lingering by the cake."

"I guess that's my cue," I offered, gathering myself up. "I can do this, right?"

"Definitely," he grinned.

The rest of the night was, as expected, a miserable trek to the finish. A leak sprung over table eleven, somebody's grandmother slipped on the soggy dance floor and maybe broke a hip, and the sparklers were too damp to stay lit for more than an anti-climatic sizzle before giving way to smoke, which isn't great for pictures. By the time I was packing up and paying out my assistants, who unsurprisingly never wanted to work with me again, Nate was bringing me a glass of champagne and a slice of decadent-looking chocolate cake.

"To this night being over," he said, raising his glass to me.

"I'll drink to that," I agreed.

I remember the way the bubbles fizzed through my chest as I smiled.

"Would you wanna meet me for brunch tomorrow morning?" he asked. "I know a place with great pancakes."

"Pancakes," I said.

"Magic pancakes, really. They can cure any kind of hangover, even the ones that aren't alcohol-induced. Everybody should try them at least once."

"Okay," I nodded.

"Okay?"

"Sure," I smiled. "I could use a little magic."

The pancakes were just okay, but his contagious conversation kept me there long after our plates were cleared. The rest, as they say, was history. In the weeks and years after that, we would laugh and thank the fates for Tyler and Brittni Marsh. We'd toast them over anniversary dinners and reminisce about them anytime the forecast called for torrential rain. We even used to joke about how we were going to invite them to our own wedding one day.

Memories like that let me know that I didn't imagine it; we'd been on the same page once, and he wanted all those things I wanted, too. Or at least he pretended to.

Maybe that's what felt the most unsettling of all: the fact that I lived with someone for two years and maybe didn't know anything about him. I saw what he wanted me to see, which was a really charismatic, likable guy that was both interesting and interested, who'd been strategically constructed with a veneer of husband material. But was any of that him? By the time he packed up his cast iron skillets and the Kitchenaid mixer, I felt like I'd been in love with someone who never even existed. And that made me feel more than a little unhinged.

"Maybe you were in love with the idea of him," Joss offered.

She had joined me on my couch, where I'd taken up permanent residence for the past week, and she'd done a respectable job at not looking too horrified when I opened the door with my swollen eyes and mismatched pajamas. I hadn't brushed my teeth since Tuesday, and I wasn't entirely sure what day it was, but I knew I was running thin on episodes of *Ru Paul's Drag Race*. My coffee table was littered with crumpled tissues and takeout containers.

"The idea of him?" I questioned.

"You know, like... when you have a celebrity crush, or a book crush, or a character in a movie you really want to bang. You can feel totally infatuated with them, even though you know they aren't really... real."

"This isn't helping."

"I'm sorry. I know," she said. "I really don't know what to say."

"There's nothing you can say. There's nothing anyone can say. It just... sucks."

"It does suck. It really fucking sucks."

"Thanks," I sighed, dropping my head to her shoulder. And I meant it, sincerely.

She squeezed an arm around me and patted my tangled hair.

"I love you," she said. "And as someone who loves you, I'm telling you you have to go take a shower."

I elbowed her with a weak laugh. She looked satisfied to have gotten a smile out of me, but I knew she was serious.

"After this episode?" I suggested.

"Deal."

She'd brought chocolates to cheer me up, and I fished one from the bag. They were the ones where the wrappers have a message on the inside, like a fortune cookie. I peeled the foil open with a glimmer of hope.

You are exactly where you are supposed to be.

Supposed to be, I scoffed.

If I was supposed to be *here*, wallowing in my shame and defeat, then I guess that means I wasn't supposed to be in a long-term relationship with that guy who didn't exist. I wasn't supposed to feel happy or hopeful about the future. I wasn't supposed to be – what would it have been at this point? – about six months pregnant. Same as my sister.

I crumpled the wrapper into a tiny silver ball and threw it into the pile of refuse on my coffee table. It bounced off a plastic cup and into the floor. Eventually, I ate the candy.

3.

Turns out, Bearded Vest Guy is at the wrong bar. He is supposed to be meeting some friends at Matty's, which is a hot wing joint on the other side of town. Somehow, it isn't closed. After he has a drink with me, he leaves. He politely invited me along, but I declined. There were a few reasons for this:

One, it was entirely too late in the evening to follow a guy all the way across town. On the zero point zero zero one percent chance it did actually snow, I didn't want to be stuck trying to get a ride back here if things didn't work out.

Two, even though it was too late to leave with him, it was also too early, as well. What if I ended up with enough extra time at the end of the night to drunk-text that asshole who is still sitting at the booth against the wall, sharing a plate of cheese fries with his friends?

Three, I wasn't getting one-night stand vibes from him. He reminded me of a Labrador Retriever puppy: cute, not totally sure of himself yet, and way too happy to be everywhere. Then there was the beard thing, and the way he smelled like he'd had quite a few shots of Fireball before he got here and looked like he planned to have quite a few more. I just wasn't feeling an instant-match-light-combustible chemistry between us.

Half of the time he was sitting beside me, I'd been trying to figure out how to work the Spark app. I definitely swiped the wrong way on a few folks. One of them sent me an eggplant emoji.

This is all okay, because there's a perfectly eligible looking bachelor in a Santa hat trying to get someone to dance with him. I'm not the biggest fan of dancing, and I don't want to look desperate, but I mean, I am. Desperate.

I give him a small smile and motion between us in the universal signal for, "Hey, you and me?"

Dancing Santa takes the bait. As Miles teases out the lyrics to "Rocking Around the Christmas Tree", Dancing Santa jives his way through the crowd and tugs me off my stool, spinning me into step with him. He's a much better dancer than me, like he belongs in an R&B video, and I do my best to keep up. One of his hands is on the curve of my waist, and though it occasionally creeps well *below* my waist, I find myself having fun.

The cymbals simmer at the end, and Miles finishes with a flair, impressively drawing out those last few notes like an old school lounge singer. He punches that last piano chord with finality as Dancing Santa dips me, eliciting whoops and whistles from the crowd, interspersed with applause.

When the music cuts for intermission, Dancing Santa escorts me back to my seat.

"Thanks for the dance," he grins. "Buy you a drink?"

He smells like cognac and cologne. I say "why not" anyway. He disappears for the restrooms in back, while the murmur of the crowd and the rattle of ice in Ari's shaker take the place of the music.

"What are you doing?" Miles asks.

He has slid in beside me again, on the stool left temporarily empty, first by Bearded Vest Guy and now by Dancing Santa. I scrunch up my eyebrows at him.

"I think I was dancing merrily, in the new old-fashioned way."

He orders a drink with a lift of his finger and returns his attention to me. My face always warms a little when he looks at me like that, like he's trying to probe the depths of my soul.

"I don't mean that. That's good for morale," he says. "What I mean is, what's up with all the guys."

I know there's no use playing coy, but still, I try.

"I'm being young and spontaneous."

He's still staring into me with a skeptical smirk.

"I am," I insist.

"That's not you," he says.

I roll my eyes. Every time I think he can't get more annoying, he raises the bar.

"You don't even know me."

"I know you enough to know that you don't want to do whatever it is you're thinking about doing."

"God, are you trying to slut shame me? Because if so, you're a fine one to talk."

He chokes on a laugh and washes it down with a sip of the drink Ari deposits in front of him, wiping his grin with the back of his hand.

"Did you just call me a slut?"

"No," I say. Then, "Maybe."

His amusement is contagious, and I'm biting into my bottom lip, trying to keep this smile from turning into something that will give him too much satisfaction.

At this moment, Dancing Santa reaches between us to retrieve his beverage. His eyes subtly dance between the two of us. I can guess what this looks like. I want Miles to stand up right then, at least give me a chance, but he only swivels halfway around and gives the guy a nod.

"Those were some good moves, Jay," he says appreciatively. "Some of your best yet."

"Hey man, you, too," Dancing Santa grins. "You guys aren't done yet, I hope?"

"No, no. Just taking a quick break. We might start taking requests in a little bit."

He's no longer looking at me at all when he nods, "Right on. You know I'm here for it. What's that new one you've been playing? Over at Metro last week?"

"'Almost Maybe Something'."

"Yeah," he says, already grooving to an imaginary beat. "Put that one on the list?"

"You got it," Miles nods.

As an afterthought, Dancing Santa nudges me and says, "Thanks again," before swaying between a couple of girls and smoothing his hands across their lower backs. I cut Miles a glance.

"Was that really necessary?"

"You should be thanking me for that."

"Because you suddenly know what's best for me?"

"No. Because I know him. And his fiancée. She's probably home right now with their two-year-old."

I open my mouth like a goldfish. Eventually I press it shut. I don't have a comeback for that. Dancing Santa is a dirty dog. Let's be real: half the guys on Spark are probably dirty dogs. Actually, worse than dogs, because dogs are at least loyal, even if they're badly in need of a bath.

"This isn't because of him, is it?" Miles asks with a visible wince. We both know, without the use of a proper pronoun, which *him* he's referring to. "Because if it is --"

"Don't you have a show to play?"

I can feel him watching me for a split second more, and I think he's going to be an asshole and keep charging down this road he veered onto, but he stands.

"Any requests?"

"Go fuck yourself," I laugh.

"A worthy proposal," he says, "but I think I prefer a partner."

I am rolling my eyes so hard when he saunters off that I think they might fall out of my head. Something about that cocky, arrogant bastard always gets under my skin. The heat has crept up my collarbones and spread down my limbs. Why couldn't he just move? Who else in our age group has lived in the same place for the past five frickin' years?

I tap my phone awake, ready to commit to whatever Spark has to offer, when I see the message from my mom.

We've got contractions! Headed to the hospital with Eleanor and Robbie now! Hopefully baby B will be here by morning!!!

I can almost hear the excitement in her voice, and suddenly all my anger is gone. I'm wearing the biggest smile of the night, brought on by the kind of joy they sing about in all those holiday jingles. Then, inexplicably, a little sadness. And a stabby shard of jealousy. And a big dose of guilt, about the jealousy. All of these mismatched feelings are spinning through my center, the way lukewarm bubblebath tornadoes down the drain.

I feel his hand squeezing my shoulder before I sense his once familiar smell: woodsmoke and sage and that fancy paste he puts in his hair. I try to steel myself before I look into his face and those gray eyes I thought I knew.

"Hey, Ceil," Nate says easily. "How ya been?"

4.

It made sense this year that I didn't go home for Christmas. My parents weren't going to be there, and Eleanor's house was going to be crowded enough. Their old guest room had been converted to a nursery, and their former office was currently housing my parents as they fully committed to #WaitingForBabyB. They packed up a week ago when Eleanor thought she was having contractions, which turned out to be gas pains, and decided it was best to stay. My mom checked in with me beforehand, complete with her concerned voice, to make sure I'd be okay on my own.

"Mom, I'm a grown woman," I said. "It'll be nice to have a quiet holiday."

I'd said the same thing when they got a great deal on a last-minute cruise over Thanksgiving. I'd declined Eleanor's repeated requests to get me to drive to Nashville and spend it with them. This was before the recent Baby Shower Incident, and the commencement of my sister and I unofficially not speaking to each other.

"But it's your first holiday, you know... of the season," she said.

I knew what she'd almost accidentally said, and I didn't fault her for it. I'd been thinking it too. This was the first year in a few that I hadn't woken up at my parents' house in fuzzy pajamas and discovered Nate coaching my dad through the process of properly roasting a turkey, per the collective wisdom of the Food Network.

"And I really want you to come!" Ellie continued. "You can help me make the dressing, and drink all this wine I can't touch, and maybe we could go see a movie, ya know, like we used to do?"

I invented a fake Black Friday shoot with four generations of a non-existent family to get out of it. I loved my sister. I thought her husband, Robbie, was pretty great. Their house and their French bulldog, Julius, were similarly adorable. As much as I wanted to see her convex and glowing, I also didn't. She was my baby sister, and for our whole lives I had always been the older, the wiser, the more experienced. In the course of a single year, though, she'd racked up a lot of big firsts, and suddenly our dynamic felt complicated. I guess that's one of those things about family; you don't always realize the roles you've been relying on until someone stops playing their part.

"But Joss will be there, right?" Mom asked.

"Yeah," I lied. "Everything's fine."

I said the same thing that April morning when I compared the instructional leaflet in the Barbie pink box to the plastic stick I was holding way too close to my face considering it was something I had peed on. I had taken it on a whim, as one does, if only to reassure myself that my missing period was just a fluke. If anything, I thought taking this test would make it show up with a vengeance, laughing at how it had faked me out, all oh-you-should've-seen-your-face. I didn't need x-ray vision to see those two pink lines staring back at me, and I didn't have to reread the box to know what they meant.

Suddenly, my Thinking Self was separated from my Blood and Bones Self, like I was stumbling through a world in which a bomb had gone off. Silence had never seemed so loud. My hands were trembling, and my stomach roiled like I might throw up, and I couldn't understand how I was still upright. My mind was everywhere but the present, to the point that I felt like I was watching someone else go through the motions of finding my phone and explaining to the receptionist at my doctor's office that I needed an appointment, any appointment, right now, today.

Everything's fine, I thought. This could be a false positive.

Everything's fine. You're twenty-eight years old. You want kids. You could figure this out.

Everything's fine. Nate loves you. No matter what.

I sat on an exam table covered with that white paper that crackles every time you move. My heart was in my stomach, like I had swallowed it whole and beating. I held my breath as the doctor strolled back into the little room.

"Well," she said. "You are pregnant."

My heart was now in my throat, like something that was coming back up. I swallowed, but it sat there. I stared at the diagram of the female reproductive system on the wall in front of me.

"How?" I finally said.

Dr. Langley studied me for a moment. "You have had unprotected sex?"

"Yes, but I'm on the pill."

I had thought about this at length. I had gone through the bathroom trash just to find the packet and confirm that I had taken them all. I took it the same exact time every single night, right after I brushed my teeth. I told her this, as coherently as possible.

"No birth control is one-hundred percent effective. Other medications can also --"

"I'm not taking any other medications," I insisted.

Her expression softened. She put her hand on my knee and gave me a patient look.

"Cecilia, I understand that this is a shock to you. I cannot explain to you how or why this happened. All I can give you are the facts."

My heart had moved into my ears, thumping loud between them. My face felt hot and prickly when I nodded. She explained what I already knew, that given the timeline, I was about five weeks pregnant, which meant I had really only become pregnant about two weeks ago. And I thought *I* was bad at math. My Thinking Self was still sorting through this, trying to remember when exactly we'd had sex that week and how many glasses of wine I'd had between then and now, while my Blood and Bones self got up, drove to the pharmacy where Joss worked, and sat with her in the parking lot.

"I can't tell him," I told her.

"You have to tell him," she said. "I mean, he'll figure it out eventually."

"Not helping."

"Sorry. But Nate. You love Nate! I'm pretty sure you've told me about a dozen times that you want to have his babies."

"We were supposed to be married first."

"Says who?" she scoffed. "That's some patriarchal bullshit and you know it."

I chewed my bottom lip as I stared across the street, where the sun glinted off cars as they rolled past. It felt strange to see people and traffic, proof that this was just another day, that life goes on, even when mine felt like it had imploded. How the hell had I managed do something by accident that people literally try for over the course of months and years? It felt like a cruelty, for me and for them, like the universe was plotting against everyone with a uterus.

"Do you want to do this?"

"I don't think I can," I admitted.

I realized that's what this feeling was: fear. Absolutely paralyzing terror. That Nate would leave. That I'd be the world's worst mom. That my family would be disappointed in me. That I'd have one of those kids who turns out to be a psychotic murderer that tortures small animals and stabs me to death in my sleep. Even Ted Bundy had a mother.

The image of Joss in her white coat blurred as I looked over. The way she squeezed my hand was the first time I'd felt whole all day.

"I know you can," she said gently. "I asked if you want to."

Turns out I did. Want to.

I ordered duck fried rice from Nate's favorite restaurant and served it on the vintage Fiestaware he inherited from his grandmother. I poured a frosty mug of his favorite IPA. I put on a cute V-neck top that was sexy and springy and decidedly not black. Everything was fine. Then the door opened.

"Today was insane," he said, shrugging out of his jacket and depositing a bag in the fridge. "Vince was hungover, Erica and Evander broke up so they're not speaking to each other, and that hurricane in the Gulf has ensured that we won't have fresh seafood for the foreseeable future. Which for a seafood restaurant is obviously not good."

He kissed me on his way around the bar.

"But Calla was testing out new dessert recipes today, so I've got some killer cake in there. You're gonna love it. You wanna know the secret ingredient? Nutmeg. Genius, right?"

He eased onto the barstool and took in the spread. Normally he cooked dinner, so this was a rare treat. I felt proud, for a moment, of my domesticity, even though I hadn't actually cooked anything.

"Oh, you got the spring rolls. You know I love the spring rolls. This is amazing, babe. Seriously, how did I get so lucky?"

He finally seemed to focus on me, a look that caught him with his beer lifted to his mouth. He lowered it to the countertop tentatively.

"Ceil? You okay?"

I took a breath. I could do this. *We* could do this.

"I'm pregnant," I said.

There it was again. That ringing, aftermath-of-an-explosion silence. I almost thought I hadn't really said anything, except for the way his face had gone slack. He was staring at me, through me, like I'd punched him in the chest.

"Say something," I whispered.

"I... uh..." he stammered. "You're...?"

The question in his eyes made me feel hopeful. I nodded. He nodded. He took a drink.

"I thought you were on..."

"I am. I was. The doctor said these things aren't a hundred percent and sometimes this just... happens."

"This just..." he said. "Wow."

"Yeah."

I felt a solidarity with that look on his face. I'd been reeling with utter shock and disbelief for most of the day, too, but seeing it reflected over dinner made me feel like it was okay that the first thing I felt wasn't joy. I actually hadn't even made it to the joy stage of this, yet. I reached across the table for him, ready to wade through these tidal emotions together. He stared at our hands, linked.

"I'm sorry, I'm just a little... surprised, is all."

"Yeah," I said, offering a relieved laugh. "Me too."

He sucked in a breath, and the next of his questions tumbled out. "Are you sure you were taking them?"

"What?"

"The birth control. The pills. You were taking them, right?"

I blinked, stunned. "What the... Yes, Nate. Of course I was taking them. Fuck."

"Okay," he said.

Distrust laced his voice. Of all the emotions I had felt today, the one rising in me was a new one. I was trembling again, but this time it wasn't fear. My words came out gasping and indignant and hot.

"That's it? Really? You think I did this on *purpose*?!"

"I don't know, Ceil," he shot back. "Fuck! What am I supposed to think?"

"I don't know! That you know me? That you know I'm not some crazy, manipulative person who would go behind your back and --"

"You're pregnant, Cecilia! People don't get pregnant by accident."

"Well I didn't get pregnant by myself!"

"So you're saying this is my fault?"

"No! I didn't say that. It's nobody's fault. It's just..."

A cruel twist of fate? A stupid fucking mistake? I didn't know how to explain it, but I knew that unfortunately there wasn't anyone to blame.

He pulled his hands through his hair so that sprigs of it fell loose from the way he always combed it smooth. He looked like an escaped criminal by the time he was done tearing at it.

"I need to..." he said, standing up. "I just need to think for a second."

He grabbed his jacket and left out the front door. Something about the way it slammed told me that it was going to be more than 'a second'. I sat there staring at the amber mug and the untouched plate. I realized I was shaking. Not just my hands this time, but a whole body shudder, like my nerves were trying to break free of my skin. I couldn't breathe. The walls felt like they were closing in on me, and all I could smell was duck fried rice, and I had to get out of this house.

I tore onto the back porch, where the cool air of early evening crept up my arms and made it obvious, by contrast, how hot my face was. I leaned over the brick-and-concrete railing and sucked in big gulps of it. I was hyper-ventilating. A few moments later, I was heaving what little was on my stomach into the grass.

My heart was broken.

I don't know how long I stood out there. Long enough that the Maine Coon cat from next door, Major Tom, wove his way around my ankles and settled onto the balustrade, with his cream-colored fur and oversized paws. This was the first time I'd seen him that he wasn't trying to dart into my place as soon as I opened the door. Normally, I found him to be even more frustrating than his human counterpart. Now, I was just grateful for his quiet presence.

Shortly after, I heard the door on the other side of the shared back porch open. I wiped my face instinctively, and only when my hand came away wet did I realize I'd been crying.

"You okay?" Miles asked.

Ever since I'd known him, it annoyed me the way his questions sounded like he'd constructed them with a period at the end. He was a shadow leaning against the stretch of railing in front of his door, like he was my own mirror image.

"I'm fine."

My voice sounded hollow.

"Not what I asked, but all right."

"Miles," I said weakly. I looked over at him now. "Not tonight."

He was watching me in that quiet way he sometimes did. It made me think of the way he looked at me the night we met, when I was standing in his doorway in pajama shorts and a t-shirt with no bra, yelling at him like a crazy person. The way he looked at me before we decided we mostly hated each other.

He nodded in understanding.

"There's always tomorrow."

It was just another one of his taunts, I was almost sure of it, but somehow it felt like more at that moment. Today had been one of those earth-shattering days. Even though it felt like there was no coming back from it, I was going to wake up in the morning and deal with it. Ready or not.

My face and fingers were numb with cold when I crawled into bed. I stared at the swirl pattern on the ceiling with my head spinning. When I heard the click of the front door, I pretended to be asleep. Nate's warmth and woodsmoke smell wrapped around me.

"I'm here," he whispered into my hair. "Ceil, I'm here. I'm sorry, I don't know what I was thinking. This is... We can do this. You and me, right?"

I rolled over to face him. His mouth was already searching out mine, kissing his way past apologies. I was so overwhelmed. I was so hurt. I was so relieved.

"Yeah," I said hoarsely. "You and me."

5.

The mood around us is downright holly-jolly. Dancing Santa is two tables away, sitting backwards in a chair like he's AC Slater, and he's about five minutes from finding my replacement. A couple of girls are leaning provocatively against Miles's piano, and I roll my eyes, wondering if I'm a few hours from figuring out if they're the subtle moan or screaming orgasm type. The post-graduate studies set has gathered at the end of the bar to wonder aloud if the coming year will finally be the one in which they defend their dissertations, and they share a round of Matilda's signature Brave Like Bruce shots, that involve hazelnut liqueur and a lemon slice, and inexplicably taste like chocolate cake.

I've got a polite smile plastered on my face. I don't know how I got sucked into his small talk. I hate small talk. One awkward hug and a few minutes of social pleasantries into it, you would think we're old pals running into each other, like maybe I used to be a friend of his sister's, or a server at his old restaurant, or a classmate he made out with at a party once but definitely never dated. This is probably what the pixie cut from Nate's booth thinks, as she glances over at us, because her smile is way too self-assured.

"I was actually thinking about you just the other day," he says. "There's this great little bodega right down the street from my apartment. It's totally your kind of place. They have the best horchata."

"Oh yeah?" I hear myself say. "That sounds... convenient."

This stupid smile I'm wearing feels very last season. It falters. The next thing I know I'm hearing about China-Mex, the food truck that he and his two business partners are planning to start, just as soon as they find the right truck and some investors who understand the genius behind their concept. This was always the story with Nate. He was perpetually a few months from launching a food vlog, or becoming a sommelier, or teaching underprivileged children how to spatchcock poultry. I used to find it endearing, and I would describe him to extended family with words like "creative" and "entrepreneurial". Now, as I'm looking at the fresh tattoo on his forearm of a whole hog, segmented into cuts of meat, like a print you might see on a butchershop wall, very different words come to mind.

"I mean, who could say no to a Szechuan chicken taco? Or queso on your fried rice?" he grins. "This could save relationships everywhere. I mean, how many couples are out there arguing right now about whether to have Chinese or Mexican? Someone should give us a peace prize."

If I had noticed it at any point before now, I could have saved myself a few years of grief and a lot of time in therapy. He's a fraud. A poseur. Do people still use the word poseur? Did that go out with Avril Lavigne? The world is his stage, and I'm just the girl sitting in the audience after having been removed from the supporting cast. I was so distracted by the husband material that I missed all the bullshit lurking beneath that carefully constructed facade. I wonder, as I look at him, if he actually believes all of his own showmanship or if it's a conscious deception.

"Anyway," he smiles. "How are your parents?"

I can't help but think about how my mom regularly asks if I've talked to him lately, like his moving to California is a long-distance phase of our relationship. Not that she got the whole story of our breakup, but I am pretty sure I did stress that it was a breakup. Maybe we all thought, on some level, that eventually he'd change his mind.

"They're doing well," I nod.

"And Eleanor? She's got to be about ready to pop by now."

Well, that is one way to put it. But no, I think. No. This is all wrong. This isn't the conversation you have with someone you semi-recently broke up with. You can say, *Hey, I miss you.* You might get bonus points for saying, *I'm really sorry.* You can even say, *I never want to see your face again.* But you cannot gleefully share how great your life is and expect me to be excited about it like we're best frickin' friends. You cannot ask about my family like they don't kind of hate your guts.

The shitty thing is I'd probably still go home with him if he asked. Something is definitely wrong with me.

"Why are you here, Nate?"

He wears that same easy expression, like he doesn't know what I mean.

"It's Christmas," he says, as if it's obvious.

"I don't mean in the city, I mean here. *Here* here. This is my bar. You never liked this bar."

"I never said that."

"Okay, I guess specifically you said the food was uninspired and the walls were too cluttered and the little lamps at all the tables were too *Good Fellas.*"

"C'mon, Ceil," he laughs.

"Don't call me that," I say. "You don't get to come in here with your tall tales from California and act like you get to call me that."

"Okay," he says.

He holds up his hands in front of him like he's fending off an assault. As if I'm the one who is being unreasonable. It's insulting. And embarrassing. I feel my face go hot enough that I'm sure it's crimson. The eternal curse of pale skin.

"I've gotta get back, but it's really good to see you, sweetie. I'll catch up with you later?"

He slips back through the crowd, and Pixie Cut smiles as he slides in beside her, and somehow the laughter and chit-chat and clinking glassware is too loud, and I can't take it anymore. I leave cash on the bar, grab my coat, and head outside. I am hit with a wave of biting cold, and I wrap myself more tightly in my scarf, wondering if I'm going to freeze to death before I make it home. The bell jingles behind me.

"Hey," Miles says. "Where are you going?"

"Home."

"There's still a fifty-fifty chance I'm going to go fuck myself. Do you really wanna miss that?"

I laugh mirthlessly.

The street is especially deserted. Most of the storefronts are dark, except for a glowing display of the Virgin Mary looking sad and serene in the thrift store window. I stare at the empty intersection, where the traffic lights cycle from green, to yellow, to red. The sky is heavy like wet wool, and I feel much the same. My eyes water, either from the wind or this feeling, and I can't look at him.

"God, it's cold out here," I say.

"Just come back inside." When I don't respond, he adds, "Are you really going to let him run you out of your own bar?"

Stubbornly, I know he has a point. I don't want to leave because of him. I don't want to stay because of him either. This must be why I'm frozen on the sidewalk.

"God, it really is cold out here," he says, shoving his hands in his pockets and shrugging his shoulders up around his ears.

"Look," he continues, "if you hang out for another hour or so, I'll drive you home."

"It's half a mile."

"It's twenty degrees out here."

I consider this. My thoughts are tangled like last year's string lights. A few of the strands aren't working, and I'm not sure which bulb is the culprit, but I'm not making much progress unraveling the knots. Realistically, I should probably throw the whole mess out and go buy more.

"He really is an asshole," I finally say.

"I've been saying this for years," he shrugs.

My face is so cold that my cheeks seem to crack open as I laugh. A truce. We've come to a few in our three-year feud. I suck in another lungful of that crisp, fresh cold. He opens the door, and we head back inside.

6.

My feud with Miles began before we even met.

It was a Monday night. With the help of a few friends with a truck and the enticement of pizza and beer, I had just moved into the other half of a Midtown bungalow that had long ago been converted into a duplex. Before this, I'd gone from my parents' house, to my college dorm, to a multi-roommate apartment, so this was the first place I was ever able to call mine.

It had a ton of character: turn-of-the-century architecture, big covered porches, and plenty of space to set up a home office where I could attempt to physically separate my work life from my personal life. I'd been reading a lot about how important it was to set those kinds of boundaries. This was going to be the place where I became that person I'd always imagined myself being: eclectic, but put-together, with a have-it-all outlook on life. I was going to eat more leafy greens, start jogging, and get a morning routine. I was going to fill my tiny closet with clothes that didn't double as something you might wear to yoga. My social media accounts were going to turn into a damn inspirational guidebook. Hashtag got this.

Then I heard the music.

I grimaced at the ceiling. I was lying in bed, the frame of which was still propped against the wall, and staring for the first night of many at the swirl pattern in the plaster above my mattress. It had to be two a.m. My moving crew hadn't cleared out until shortly after midnight, and I'd spent at least an hour trying to unpack my kitchen and make sure when I woke up in the morning I knew where to find my silverware and favorite mug so I could make the Pinterest-worthy latte that was going to fuel all of my elaborate morning-person dreams.

Who played music like this at two a.m.? Not the hip-hop hits or pop country anthems that plagued my old place, where our building was literally across the street from a frat house, but piano music. It wasn't classical, like Bach or Beethoven, but it was beautiful. And loud.

I groaned. I didn't want to be that neighbor. I was new here. I considered that maybe whoever was on the other side hadn't realized anyone had moved in. And this couldn't go on forever, right?

I rolled into the fetal position and pulled the blankets tightly over my head. A little while later I added a pillow, wondering if I might accidentally smother myself before I could fall asleep. My eyes were dry and heavy when I checked the time again. It was three o'clock. The witching hour. The famed time of songs about how we can't help but be scared of it all sometimes. The time that most decent people were quiet and sleeping.

I was mentally rehearsing how I was going to go over there and calmly ask the after-midnight pianist to stop, even though that was very quit-with-your-rock-music and get-off-my-lawn and sign-me-up-with-AARP, when everything went silent. I perked up, listening for a few breaths before sinking against the mattress in a long sigh of gratitude. I offered up words of praise for multiple deities. Relief settled in me the way a dog circles twice before curling onto that perfect spot on the couch. I had already rolled onto a comfy position on my stomach, with the pillows just right and one foot outside the covers, ready to succumb to sweet, perfect sleep, when that same damn song started again.

I shot upright and launched my pillow across the room.

"What the actual fuck," I growled into the dark.

The polite girl I imagined I would be had disappeared two or three songs ago. I threw off the blankets, stomped barefoot across the shared porch to the front door beside mine, and banged against the heavy wood until I thought pieces of the old paint might chip off. I wasn't even trying to be quiet, since whoever was over here clearly wasn't sleeping. I waited with my arms folded angrily across my chest. No response.

"Seriously?" I said to myself. Then louder, "Hello? Can you hear me? Open up!"

I beat against the door like I was trying to hammer my message home. I was putting so much force into it I almost fell inside when it opened. A guy stood in front of me, wearing athletic shorts, an oversized cable knit sweater, and a thoroughly bewildered expression.

"Do you have any idea what time it is?" I demanded.

His eyes were wide, and he seemed to be taking me in in pieces: my tossing-and-turning hair, my lack of footwear, and the scowl on yesterday's made-up face. He glanced around like I might have a posse with me.

"Hey. Yeah, it's um... Are you okay? Do you need me to call someone?"

"What?" I stammered.

"The cops or... a friend, maybe?"

"*What?*" I repeated, twisting up my face in confusion. "No! I need you to stop with the goddamn music."

The confusion was contagious, and now it was his turn to blink indignantly and ask, "Wait, what?"

"I'm your neighbor," I explained. "I live next door."

Realization was dawning. It swept across him, easing that furrowed brow and tight jaw into an expression that was young and smirky and slightly amused. Okay, definitely amused. He pulled a hand through his dark hair before dragging it across his face.

"Are you laughing?" I asked.

He was definitely laughing. He leaned against the doorframe, like he required assistance holding himself up.

"I thought you were, like, an escaped kidnap victim or something."

Now it was my turn to look dumbfounded. I stood there, pulling myself up to my full height, which still put me half a head shorter than him. I narrowed my stare.

"Are you serious right now?"

He was trying unsuccessfully to wipe that ridiculous grin off his face. Eventually, he extended a hand.

"Sorry. I'm sorry. I'm Miles."

"Cecilia," I said warily.

I felt annoyed, and exhausted, and beyond ready for this interaction to be over. I slid my hand out of his.

"Could you just... keep it down?"

"Yes. I'm sorry. I didn't know you were... The landlord didn't say... I'm in a band."

I rolled my eyes though he couldn't see it. I was already retreating to my door.

"Of course you are," I mumbled.

"I'm really glad you weren't kidnapped," he called after me. "Can I get a do-over on this?"

"Good night, Miles," I called back.

Later that fall, when Nate moved in, we would have a few more run-ins. Sometimes it was the noise, a few times it was backyard parties, and once I might have called the cops on him. I wasn't especially proud of that particular moment. Often it was the issue of his daredevil cat trying to sneak into my place, which occasionally resulted in my discovering him curled up in a basket of clean laundry or lying across my computer keyboard a few hours after hauling in my groceries.

"Could you keep him inside?" I asked, passing the oversized fluff-ball back to him for the third time that week. It was always worse in the fall.

"Why would he wanna be stuck at my place when he can be over there with you?"

"Ugh," I groaned, stalking away.

"Good talking to you."

What single guy who wasn't attempting to become an internet sensation even owned a cat, anyway?

Then there was the months-long episode we referred to as The Recycle Bin Situation, in which Nate had become convinced that Miles was putting his empty bottles and discarded plastics into our curbside receptacle.

"I think he's doing it on purpose, Ceil. It's just laziness. He doesn't want to walk his bin out to the curb."

"I thought I saw his bin on the curb."

"Well maybe it's full, in which case he should reduce his consumption. No single person should be able to fill up a whole bin in a week."

"What am I supposed to do about it?" I asked. "Do you want me to talk to him?"

"No, no," he said. "I'll handle it."

Miles wasn't home during the day, and Nate wasn't home many nights, so he'd written a note and taped it to Miles's window. The next evening, Nate stormed in with the paper in hand, waving it around like it was the 95 Theses he'd just ripped from our door. I could see the red ink from across the room.

"What's wrong?" I demanded, half in a panic.

"He corrected the grammar and gave it back," Nate raved. "Fuck this guy!"

In hindsight, it was kind of hilarious, because Nate did have a cringe-worthy tendency to use the wrong your/you're. At the time, however, it had meant war.

The thing that really solidified how I felt about Miles, though, happened the second week I knew him.

"I'm having a party Friday night," he said. "And I know you have an eight o'clock curfew, being seventy-five and all, but I think you should come."

I smiled. We had spoken a few times in daylight, after I'd gotten some rest and had some coffee, and things had gone significantly better. The fact that there hadn't been any more noise complaints definitely helped.

"What's the occasion?"

"Last day of school celebration."

I studied him for a moment, wondering if I'd misjudged his age. He had an affinity for band t-shirts that would rival a teenager's, and there was something boyish about his face, but he had a filled out look to him that you don't find in guys under twenty-five. Those were definitely man shoulders.

"You're in college?"

"Briarwood Middle. I teach music. And English. And sometimes when they're really short on funding, US History."

"A man of many talents," I observed.

"Don't look so impressed. And don't ask me about anything that happens after the American Civil War because we've never gotten that far," he laughed. "Anyway, this next couple of weeks is the very short window when I get to relax a little. I travel a lot during the summer. The band has a few festivals lined up, and we usually drop into some of the smaller venues in the bigger cities."

"Like a tour?"

"Sort of."

"Hm. Am I allowed to be impressed about that?"

"Oh yeah, that's totally why I do it," he smirked. "So you'll swing by?"

"Maybe," I shrugged.

I didn't need that tingly feeling spreading under my skin to know I really liked Miles. He was cute, and I have a weakness for cute guys. But he also looked like the kind of guy who knew he was cute. Add that to the fact he was a musician, and that likelihood increased exponentially. I'm also pretty sure it was a law of the universe that it was a bad idea to develop a crush on your neighbor. As such, My Thinking Self knew whatever happened with us in the future needed to remain platonic. My Blood and Bones Self, though, was a shifty bitch who convinced me to slather myself in my favorite scented lotion, shimmy into a cute pair of jeans, and curl my hair into sassy, shoulder-length mermaid waves before I headed over that evening.

The layout of his place mimicked mine, but while mine was tidy to the point of looking sparse, his was filled with lamps, rugs, art, books, and an old upright piano topped with a cream-colored cat, who wasn't at all bothered by the two dozen or so people spilling out into the backyard. A fire pit had crackled to life about an hour earlier, and a guy with a long beard and a felt hat was strumming a guitar. I was wandering towards the open back door, plotting my next move, when his words crept up behind me.

"I don't believe we've met."

I was smiling before I even turned around. He looked entirely too good in his jeans and t-shirt, perched on the edge of his kitchen counter. Like he'd been waiting for me. I bit the inside of my bottom lip.

"Cecilia," I offered. "Neighbor. Not kidnapped. And you are?"

That hint of a smile played across his face.

"Really glad you came."

I never went for this: this playful banter, and those guys who never take anything seriously. When his teasing eyes flicked across my features, my heart flipped anyway.

"I said I would."

"You said you might. Did you decide to Tivo *60 Minutes?*"

"You're really making me question my decision, here."

He hopped off the counter. "Can I get you a drink?"

"I heard something about margaritas?"

"Sure. But I'm gonna warn you, I only make them two ways: strong and extra strong."

"Strong, please. And salt?"

"Oh yeah. Salt's a must."

He passed me a glass and made introductions. His friends were an easy group to fall in with, the kind of people who had never met a stranger, and within no time I had made lunch plans with Jenna, realized I had mutual connections with Tavian, and become entangled in a riotous game of Pictionary with Patrick, Espe, and the crowd filling up the mismatched sofas, armchairs, and ottomans in the living room. It was delightfully distinct from all those beer-pong-ridden post-college parties I still occasionally found myself at, and I felt an instant sense of belonging here, among these pseudo-adults with our big aspirations and fledgling careers.

It was one of those nights that gets away from you, and somewhere between the bottomless margaritas and good conversation, it was one in the morning. It had gotten cooler around midnight, but not enough to warrant heading inside. It was one of those nights that made you never want to go inside.

Everything was blooming, and even through the smoky embers you could smell the damp earth and hints of honeysuckle. Half of everyone had gone home, but I was perched on the balustrade of the back porch, nursing my drink and watching the stragglers left around the dying fire, who were intermittently arguing about wild, political conspiracy theories.

"Think we should stop them?" I asked as their voices escalated.

The retro string lights edging the roof of the back porch glowed above us, and I could feel Miles's warmth against my knee as he leaned against the column.

"Eh. I think we've got about half an hour before we're in danger of the band breaking up, at which point I guess I'll step in."

"Probably prudent. Speaking of the band, you know the actual saying is 'the devil's in the details', right?"

He laughed. "Yes. Occasional English teacher, remember? It sounds remarkably similar when you say it, though, and it felt really clever in our first year of college."

"Mm. Another attempt to impress all the girls?"

"Are you impressed?"

I took a swig of my drink, unwilling to dignify this with a reply. We'd had enough tequila that our smiles felt smooth and syrupy, and I pulled my gaze back out into the night, hoping to quiet that thrill rising within me.

"Irregardless," I said, dragging out the syllables. "It's not the same."

If he was trying to hide that smile, he failed miserably. "It pretty much is, for all intensive purposes."

I laughed. This felt dangerously close to flirting. Did it count as flirting if you were doing it in commonly misused phrases? Did it get any more ridiculous than this? The answer to both of those was *yes, probably.* Somehow, that didn't stop me from adding, "I think maybe that's proof you're just a pre-Madonna."

This time, he laughed. He lifted his drink to that playful smile.

"You know I could care less what you think."

"Oh yeah? How much less?"

My pulse simmered, and his eyes flickered with amusement. I knew this hopeless smile was probably giving me away. I couldn't even blame the tequila.

"I know what you're doing," he said. "You're getting me back for the other night."

"I've mostly forgiven you for that."

"Really." He smirked, like he didn't believe me.

"I think so. As long as you don't make it a habit of playing your rock music after midnight, young man."

"See, the thing is, if I know you'll come running to my door every time I do it, I don't know that it's the best incentive for me to stop."

"Mm, no," I said, shaking my head slowly. Even as I did this, I bit into my bottom lip. *Damn, he was cute.* "Your lines won't work on me."

"Ah. You're impervious to my charm?"

"I'm your neighbor."

He watched me for a few moments with that focused gaze, but to his credit, he didn't try to act like he didn't know what I meant.

"Right," he admitted.

"Sorry," I shrugged.

"You're not planning on moving anytime soon? I hear the guy who lives here is a real asshole. Loud. Obnoxious. Terrible taste in music."

It was an involuntary thing, the way I leaned into him a little as I laughed. He reached out instinctively, grazing my arm like he was worried I might fall. And suddenly, I was too. He was too cute, and too warm, and we were too close. I felt like I could fall in love with him without a second thought, and that just wasn't me. I had just met him. I needed time to overthink things, time to investigate him on the internet and weigh the pros and cons.

His gaze traced along my smile. That feeling tugging through me let me know I should stumble the ten feet home before I did something I might regret.

"We should probably set some boundaries," he suggested, as if reading my mind. Even as he said this, he reached up and threaded one of my curls around his fingers. Slowly. He was careful not to brush my skin, but chills ran across my collarbone anyway. My gaze slid up to his.

"Boundaries are good," I agreed.

"So... no touching?"

I could still feel his hand in my hair, just close enough to my neck to send that tingling awareness spreading further across my skin. I met his questioning gaze with a knowing glance. It killed me to say it.

"Probably not."

He nodded, letting his hand slip away just as easily, but his gaze held steady.

"And... no flirting?"

I pressed into my smile. How did he do that? It's like a switch he could flip, and my chest went all tingly, and my mouth crept up at the corners. I shook my head, and definitely blamed the tequila this time, but I didn't put any distance between us.

"Mm-mm. Flirting is absolutely forbidden."

"And definitely no kissing."

He said it matter-of-factly, like he knew it was already decided, but his eyes danced across my face, my mouth, that brush of hair falling across my shoulders. This was the first time of many that he would look at me like that, like he was running his fingers along the edges of all my little details, like those eyes could slip into my soul and pull out all my secrets.

Neighbor, I reminded myself. *Ridiculously bad idea.*

But god, I wanted to. I wanted to kiss him, wanted to stay up all night talking about everything and nothing. My reply was just an exhale.

"Can I... get back to you on that?" I murmured.

His response was as slow and warm as the wave of wanting that swept through me.

"Sure. Can I at least walk you home?"

I laughed, sliding off my perch and onto my buzzed legs. My hand fell against his chest as I steadied myself, and I let it linger for a moment, fighting the urge to lean into him.

"I think I got it," I replied. "See you tomorrow?"

I felt him smiling as I walked away, a small satisfaction that I would still be reveling in as I lay in bed, thinking about how I might break all my rules for him. The no musicians mandate, and the no self-satisfied smirky guys clause, and even that well-known idiom about not shitting where you sleep, or where you eat, or whatever it was.

"You never told me," I said, pausing at my door, "what it meant. The devils and the details."

"Next time."

That smile spread through me like a promise. The tingle of anticipation was still coursing through me when I woke up the next morning. I thought about him as I showered, and made my coffee, and outlined all the move-in chores I still needed to do. I was even singing to myself while I worked, like some sort of cartoon princess.

It was only a few hours later, while I was hanging curtains, that I saw her leaving in last night's clothes: Jenna.

I sank to my stepladder, drill in hand, and watched as she smiled over her shoulder at him. She was blowing him kisses and laughing across her goodbyes as the heat spread across my face, and I felt like such an idiot. I realized then that he was the kind of guy who would settle for anyone, when I wouldn't settle for being anything less than *the* one. I couldn't believe how close I'd been, and I knew I wouldn't make that mistake again.

7.

Is it snowing yet?

Joss's message catches me just as I slide begrudgingly back onto my designated barstool, right in front of an annoyed looking man who has been eyeing the seat.

"See?" Ari says to him. "I told you. She just went outside to take a call."

He rolls his eyes and weaves back into the crowd.

"Thanks for that," I offer.

"I'm glad you came back," she grins. "I am not in the mood to deal with shitty pickup lines."

"Hey, if you keep pouring me these drinks, no promises," I say. "Things could get weird."

She laughs, and I feel my mood lightening. As if they've been saving it for just this moment, The Devils & the Details return strong with "Let It Snow". The whole place, as expected, becomes a riotous chorus. People are way too into this.

LOL, I reply to Joss. *No. But hell might be freezing over. I'm thinking about getting a ride home with my asshole neighbor. Tell me it's a bad idea.*

Joss's message is a series of emojis: gasping, laughing, and one where the little multi-colored brain explodes.

Yeah right, she replies. *That sounds about as likely as the winter wonderland they've predicted. But seriously, you should do it.*

She follows up with a winky face and a little devil icon. This is our running joke, that if I operate as the eternal voice of reason, she is the devil on our shoulders feeding us questionable ideas. It was her duty, she always said, to bring balance to my forces of good. I reply with an angel and pocket my phone.

I wish she was here.

I swear I have other friends. It's not like Joss is the only person I can count on. The sad truth is this is what happens when you're almost thirty: Jade got a fellowship and moved to Phoenix, Alex married a guy none of us can stand and started calling herself Alexandra, and Talia has three kids and probably passed out in yesterday's clothes with a copy of *Goodnight Moon* across her face a few hours ago. We still talk, but they're not the people I can summon out on a whim.

That's the best part about sitting at the bar, though: nobody questions why I'm alone. Unless you're the short, twenty-five-year-old with a '70s porn star mustache easing up beside me when the pair of grad students previously sharing that single barstool relocates.

"Is your boyfriend sitting here?" he asks.

"No," I reply.

"Cool," he says, taking a swig of his drink. "Do you have a boyfriend, though?"

I don't, obviously, have a boyfriend, but I do have this issue of not being able to control my facial expressions when someone asks me stupid questions. I grimace.

"Don't do that."

"Excuse me?" he says, straining to hear me over the music.

"Don't sit there," I say, a bit louder.

I wonder, at this moment, where the angry bald guy went. I would gladly offer him the seat. I also wonder when I became this bitter bitch, the girl who verbally assaults ex-boyfriends and mustached-looking hobbits a few days before Christmas. He is giving me a look now that's remarkably similar to the one Nate gave me earlier, and he rolls his eyes before sauntering off. A beanie-wearing bro who thankfully has no interest in chatting with me briefly takes his place.

The band is mixing in originals with the Christmas songs now, which is a welcome relief, and I have to admit they're actually pretty good. I sip my drink and sift through Spark, which has turned into more of a social curiosity than a serious conquest, since all the prospects either have poorly-cropped, unflattering pictures, or grammatically incorrect taglines, or gym-mirror-selfie abs. I'm half-horrified, half-fascinated, and almost enjoying myself, when Ari brings me a shot I didn't order. I raise an eyebrow in question. She tosses her head over to that infamous booth, and when I catch Nate's eye, he gives me an apologetic smile across the way. *Forgive me?* it says. As if copious amounts of alcohol could erase everything between us.

When he said "I'll catch up with you later", I assumed he meant it in the general sense. The hope in his eyes, though, seems to indicate something more probable, like later this weekend, or later tonight.

I slide the glass towards me. It's milky and cold, and I wonder if it's one of those that tastes just like Cinnamon Toast Crunch. He knows I like those, and how they call them Saturday Morning Cartoons on the menu. I make a show of picking it up, the way you might imagine an infomercial starlet showing off merchandise, and I smile. Then I proceed to pour it out, straight into the slotted narrow drain under the beer taps in front of me. I pass the empty to Ari on her way by, and when I look over again, he's doing his best impression of someone who hasn't noticed.

***

"What about the name Ewan?" Nate suggested, pulling a frittata from the oven.

"As in, McGregor?" I asked.

"There are other Ewans."

"Name one."

He thought for a moment, adding two pieces of bacon to my plate.

"I think it's cool," he retorted.

"You do realize there's a fifty-fifty chance it's a girl, right? And we've got like eight months to settle on a name?"

"Let me have my dreams, okay?"

His stubble scraped across my forehead as he kissed me. He deposited a cup of coffee in front of me, along with a plate. He had gotten really serious about the making-it-up-to-me mission, and it had been two weeks of being well-fed and doted on, complete with foot rubs while we watched TV and fancy breakfast every morning. A girl could get used to this.

I smiled, taking a sip of my coffee. Watery bitterness filled my mouth, and I swallowed it begrudgingly.

"Is this... decaf?" I grimaced.

"Babe," he said. "Do you want our kid to come out jonesing for an espresso?"

I eyed the mug as if he'd just served me poison. Poison I was actually considering drinking, given the alternative of no hot beverage at all. I imagined myself, a few months from now, hiding in my car and sucking down Starbucks, then discarding the evidence in Miles's recycle bin. I'd have to start giving the baristas a fake name, too, just in case anyone got suspicious. Was my fight for bodily autonomy really going to commence with lattes?

"That's okay," I said, standing up. "I've got a shoot across town I need to get to."

"You want me to pack this to-go?"

"That'd be great," I grinned.

I ate the frittata in the car while I drove with my knees, running notes through my mind about lighting and composition from my scouting expedition. I knew, though, that those cherry blossoms would already look different now than they did a few days ago. I was booked for sessions through late afternoon, preparing myself for crying toddlers, couples in which one person really hated taking pictures, and that family whose GoldenDoodle always tried to hump my leg. There wasn't a hint of sarcasm in telling myself it was going to be a great day. The sky was blue, the trees were a fantasy-world of white and pink blooms, and I was in love.

With the morning sessions behind me and the afternoon closing in, I bought a sandwich from a nearby food truck and sat on the curb, warming myself in the sun like a cat. I would think about this moment a lot in the coming months. Everything that followed could have gone so many ways. I could have carried on, drinking decaf coffee and enjoying early morning frittatas. I could have fought with Nate over how there was no way we were naming our hypothetical son Ewan. I could have gone to my appointment the following week and seen a little gummy bear of an image on the ultrasound screen. Instead, I felt that uncomfortable rush that every woman is familiar with, like your body has turned on the cervical fluid faucet or you're about to be in desperate need of some feminine products.

I took one of those subtle peeks at my pants and comforted myself with the idea it was a false alarm. This was fine. This was probably one of those pregnancy things I'd have to get used to. I finished my lunch, did the afternoon sessions, and headed home. Then I saw all that bright red, and I crumpled to the floor, along with all those other imaginary plans.

If I'd been upset that my doctor hadn't been able to give me a good reason for the pregnancy, the fact that she couldn't explain the miscarriage was even more devastating. Was it the ham sandwich? Was it the birth control, there at the beginning? Was it the sex we'd had last week? Was my body an inhospitable place, incapable of this basic biological function that is so easy for some people to accomplish they literally make TV shows about how teenagers can do it?

"These things happen," Dr. Langley said. "Sometimes we don't know why. It's very likely that you'll go on to have successful pregnancies in the future."

I lay in bed, feeling more like a failure than I'd ever felt. Nate brought me food I never ate and turned on TV shows I didn't pay attention to. We hadn't really told anyone, so there wasn't anyone to tell about this turn of events. And there also wasn't anyone to comfort us, which was probably for the best. I knew how people typically handled things like this.

"God has a plan."

"There was probably something wrong with the baby."

"It's not like you guys were really trying, anyway."

"At least it was early."

I made up imaginary arguments over these topics with people I passed on the street or saw in line at the grocery store. I referred a newborn session to a colleague of mine and started unfollowing every friend who posted pictures of their babies on social media. The shitty thing about grief is that it's quiet. It creeps up when you're sitting at a stoplight, or doing laundry, or seeing your sister's perfectly Pinterested pregnancy announcement splashed all over the internet. Meanwhile, all around you, life carries on.

"I'm just having a hard time, Nate."

"You're always having a hard time lately."

"We lost our baby. *I* lost our baby."

"This again? Ceil, you have to get over this. It's over, done. We don't have a baby. You were barely even pregnant."

It was an immediate reaction: my stomach twisted, my mouth fell open wide, and my blood was turned up all the way to boil.

"Um, no. I was definitely pregnant."

"Were you? There was no heartbeat, no ultrasounds, no nothing. For all I know you made this whole thing up."

I blinked at him, stunned. His arms were folded across his chest, and he was giving me this look of superiority. Like he had figured it all out. Like he was right. Betrayal laced my words.

"There were blood tests, and…"

And blood, I thought. Thick, dark, heart-wrenching buckets of it. That was all definitely real, even if the future I had imagined full of binkies and bottles and a neutral color scheme nursery was not.

"You think I made this up? Who would… I can't even… Why would I do that, Nate?"

"To trap me? To get me to marry you? I don't know!"

My face stung like I'd been slapped. The anger was receding, replaced by an impossible hurt.

"I didn't think I had to trap you." The words were hoarse to the point of being a whisper. "I thought you wanted to be here."

"I do," he said. Then, "I did. Shit, I don't know. You're not the same."

I couldn't argue with that. I wasn't the same. I stood there staring until he shook his head and stalked out of the room. We didn't talk for two days. When we finally did, we never brought it up again.

***

Yeah. Fuck him.

Maybe it was a delayed reaction for me, because I didn't come to that conclusion until August, after he left. I was standing in my kitchen, trying to make macaroni and cheese, when I realized I didn't have a strainer. I dug through the cabinet where it usually resided, fuming.

That was *my* strainer.

I'd bought it for my multi-roommate apartment, long before I ever met Nate. It was a bright pink plastic that wasn't fancy or expensive and couldn't have at all been mistaken for anything of his. But it wasn't here. You know what was, though? A stray piece of Fiestaware. It was a yellow serving dish, oblong and heavy, from the collection he'd carted off to California. I pulled it from beneath the pitcher I used in the summer to make mojitos and stared at it.

I'm not sure what possessed me. I'm also not sure which came first: the guttural scream or the overhand motion that sent it flying against the wall. It all happened so fast. Maybe it had actually splintered when it hit the tile, not necessarily when it hit the drywall, where it had left a slight indentation. Regardless, sharp yellow pieces of it were spread out across my entire living space, like I'd shattered the midday sun. My pulse was throbbing in my ears, followed closely by knocking at my back door.

"Cecilia?"

I groaned. I didn't want a witness for this, but I reasoned he might call the cops if I didn't say anything, possibly imagining me bludgeoned over the head by an intruder and lying unconscious on the floor. I was barefoot as I trudged over and unlatched the door.

"Hey," I said casually.

"Hey," Miles returned, peering in behind me. "Are you okay? I thought I heard a scream."

"Yeah," I offered, with a steadying breath. "I... dropped a plate."

I could tell by the look on his face he didn't exactly believe me, but it was followed quickly by, "Holy shit, you're bleeding."

"What?"

I followed his gaze to the bloody footprint I'd left when I shifted. Suddenly, everything came into sharp focus.

"Oh god," I breathed.

When the door opened further, he took in the remnants of the serving dish, spread in such a way that nobody would ever believe I had simply dropped the thing. His shoes crunched as he took a tentative step inside.

"Um, do you need help?"

"Clearly."

"Where's your broom? I can try to clear you a path to the couch."

"I don't know if I still have one," I admitted.

"How do you not have a broom?"

"Nate moved out."

Miles hadn't yet returned from his usual summer excursion when the big metal moving pod showed up out front, so I figured he might be a little behind. The dumbfounded look on his face let me know that had been an accurate assumption.

"Oh," he said. "Like, *moved out* moved out or..."

"Miles," I said. "I'm bleeding. Can we discuss this when I no longer have a piece of Fiestaware in my foot?"

"Yeah, okay."

He attempted to kick a few shards to the side before sweeping a hand through his hair. "I can carry you to the couch?"

I grimaced. He gave me a look.

"Do you have any better ideas?" he challenged.

My foot was starting to sting a little, and the prospect of adding to the issue was not favorable. I rolled my eyes to the ceiling and sighed. "Fine."

After a few false starts, his arm snaked around me, and he scooped me up in a search-and-rescue kind of way. Suddenly, the thought of being carried across my apartment by him in this particular configuration was too much.

"Okay, okay. Not like that," I said.

He lowered my feet to the floor with a frustrated breath. It was clear I needed to get across the room, but the look we were exchanging -- the questioning one in which his gaze traveled me up-and-down -- let me know that his next line of thinking was to hoist me up and wrap me around him, front-to-front. My wince turned to a scowl.

"No," I protested. "Absolutely not."

His arms fell to his sides.

"How else am I supposed to do it?"

"Maybe you can turn around and I can just ride on your back," I offered.

He shot me a skeptical glance but eventually agreed. I launched myself onto his back with my arms clutched around his neck and my legs wrapped around his middle, like a graceless spider monkey. When his hands hooked under my thighs, I realized this particular configuration was probably worse than the fireman carry. I was pressed into his back with my chin over his shoulder, hyper-aware that this was as close as I'd been to him, like, ever. He smelled really, really good. Intoxicatingly good. I was caught somewhere between wanting to suck in big gulps of it and hold my breath as we clumsily headed for the sofa.

"You're choking me," he said halfway, pausing to readjust.

"Sorry," I sighed.

When he deposited me on the couch, I propped my foot up on the coffee table so he could inspect. It was strange seeing him in my place, on his knees, with his hand on my ankle. His brows knitted together in concern.

"Don't look at it like that," I said.

"Like what?"

"Like you're considering amputation. It's freaking me out."

"I just need some gloves. And tweezers. Do you have a first

aid kit?"

"I mean, I don't even have a broom, so..."

He gave me a pointed look before sighing his way toward the front door.

"You're just going to leave me like this?"

"I'll be right back," he replied. "Don't move."

Like I could if I wanted to, I thought.

When he disappeared, I took a moment to run a hand through my hair before feeling ridiculous. This is what my life had become: getting self-conscious because a guy touched my ankle. A guy I didn't even like. I folded my arms across my chest to prevent any more preening. I needed a distraction.

Wait, what the hell was I saying? I was bleeding. The stinging pain was supposed to be the distraction. I dropped my head back against the couch and stared at the ceiling. A few minutes later, he returned with a first aid kit and a dustpan.

"Tell me how you managed this again," he said.

His hand held gentle pressure against my foot as he doused the cuts in peroxide. I made a face.

"I dunno," I offered. "The damn thing just exploded."

"Well, that's certainly what it sounded like," he laughed.

I let my head drop back against the sofa. "We really need thicker walls."

"Seriously," he agreed. "I'm lucky that thing didn't fly straight into my living room and clock me in the head."

I gave him a look. His smirk flicked up at me before focusing again. He was picking three slivers of ceramic out of my foot when I noticed that the burgundy polish on my big toe was chipped and wondered when I last had a pedicure. And also when I last shaved my legs. Not that this was a time for vanity.

"Thanks," I offered. "For your help."

"No problem. Just being neighborly." Then, "I'm sorry about Nate."

Despite the pain shooting up my leg, I broke into a laugh.

"What?" he questioned.

"I'm just amazed you said that with a straight face."

His eyes flickered with amusement before returning to the extraction process.

"What happened?"

That was the million dollar question, wasn't it?

"It just didn't work out."

"Obviously," he deadpanned, dropping another piece of shrapnel onto the coffee table. "I meant why."

I mulled it over, thinking about the dozen ways I could explain it. I didn't want to tell him about the food truck, or the miscarriage, or the way we hadn't had sex in three months. I was still too emotional and honestly a little embarrassed, even though that didn't make any logical sense. Was a breakup actually embarrassing? When I thought about what a fool I'd been for believing his big charade, I decided... yes. Eventually, I just sighed.

"That bad, huh?" he said.

"Yeah," I nodded.

"Breakups can be brutal. Once, a girl broke up with me at a Chili's."

I laughed in spite of myself.

"Why were you at Chili's to begin with?"

"They have that appetizer thing – the triple dipper? Anyway, that's not important," he smiled. "This other one left me in the middle of a tour for the drummer in one of the opening acts. That one really ended with a bang, if you know what I mean."

"Oh my god. How many of these do you have?"

"I haven't even told you about the girl who left me for the horseback riding instructor."

"What horseback riding instructor?"

"The one that led us on the romantic ride around a lake, that I'd planned for her birthday. Turns out it was way more romantic for them than for us."

"You're making this up."

"I'm not," he defended. "His name was Graham. I'm pretty sure they got married."

"Ouch," I said. "How'd you get over it?"

"The same way Taylor Swift does. I wrote a breakup album."

We were both smiling as he pulled off the gloves and left the tweezers on the table.

"All done," he said. "Want me to help you clean this up before you hurt yourself again?"

"No," I insisted. "I've got it. You've done enough. I'll return your dustpan tomorrow?"

"Sure," he nodded. "And, uh, just yell if you need anything?"

I laughed, rolling my eyes. He was still too cute, and too warm, and too close. He was also still my neighbor.

When he opened the door to leave, Major Tom darted in. He was halfway to the kitchen when Miles caught him. He carried him against his shoulder like a sour-faced infant and offered me an apologetic grin.

"Thanks," I said again. This time, I actually smiled.

After he left, I swept up the mess and ate soggy macaroni. The next afternoon, I came home to a broom with a big red bow tied to the handle, waiting by my door.

8.

MY SISTER IS DILATED TO THREE.

As much as I don't need the play-by-play of her cervix – or anyone's cervix, ever, for that matter – it brings with it an undercurrent of excitement, similar to the energy of all these perfect strangers swaying in unison to the chorus of "The Lights and Buzz". To Miles's credit, he changes the line about "Christmas in California" to "Christmas here at Matilda's", and it warms my soul, especially since Nate's relocation has converted me to the "Aenima" stance on the state, as in I've hoped more than a few times it would break off into the ocean. My mood soars with the melody.

Regulars at Matilda's are always an interesting sort, and even with tonight's pre-holiday desperation crowd, I can easily spot them. They're young professionals who live in the neighborhood, middle-aged professionals who never found it in their hearts to move out to the suburbs, and messy-haired stoners who occasionally show up in their pajamas. By the last set, I've made friends with a couple who snagged the seats beside me. I recognize one by her cat-eye glasses and the other by his fabulous fedora.

"Happy Solstice, honey!" Cat Glasses tells me.

"It's good to see a familiar face in here!" Fabulous Fedora says. "Can you believe all this nonsense about snow? People will believe anything."

"These people don't even know what they're hoping for!" she complains. "I was here in '94 during the ice storm. The streets froze, the power lines snapped, the pipes in my kitchen burst."

Fabulous Fedora laughs, remembering.

"No power?" I say. "How did *you* not freeze?"

"Body heat," she replies, waggling her dramatic eyebrows.

We share a laugh and clink our glasses together. I don't know why I'm toasting, but it feels right, somehow. I decide, with Cat Glasses and Fabulous Fedora swaying beside me and singing along, that it *is* good to be alive. We're about to have a baby; the first boy in our family since my dad, if the ultrasounds are to be believed. I've also got enough gigs lined up that I might not be scraping by to cover all my bills this month, like I have almost every one since Nate left. Everything feels hopeful.

Miles's hands work effortlessly across the piano keys, and the melody slows as he leans into the microphone. That sweep of hair falls across his forehead.

"Thanks for ditching your families and hanging out with us tonight," he says, and the crowd laughs. "Merry Christmas to y'all, and to y'all a good night."

It leaves me with that warm nostalgic feeling, like the end of a children's book, and brings with it a flurry of people finishing their beverages, paying their tabs, and sliding into their coats. Cat Glasses gives me an air kiss on each cheek, and Fabulous Fedora offers me a festive wink. The place feels half empty within minutes.

This is when Nate strolls up to me in his short sleeves. I notice

Mark Twain's face on his tricep, and I wonder when it was added and why, because an educated guess tells me he's never read a single line about Tom Sawyer or Huck Finn.

"Hey," he smiles. "I think we're gonna get out of here. Hannah was telling us about this speakeasy that serves late-night tapas."

When I don't reply he says, "I mean, it's not China-Mex, but..."

I realize he's inviting me. My laugh is an involuntary thing that bubbles up through my chest. I'm trying to figure out what version of events he has told himself to make bringing me along seem like a good idea. And I wonder what's going on with the Pixie Cut – *Hannah* – and if she knows we used to live together. Given the fact that *he* doesn't even seem to know we used to live together, I'm going to assume not. Would they be inviting me along if she knew? Or is this a pity invite altogether?

There's a stabby jealous part of me that wants to claim him for the night just so she can't have him. There's an even sadder part of me that wants to drag him into bed and have him whisper against my skin that he's sorry he ever left, what the hell was he thinking. In that scenario, there's a vindictive streak that also wants to crush him and say I only ever used him, and an alternate version that wants to welcome him back and settle into the way things were. My feelings are so fragmented. This night, this entire year, has left me emotionally splintered.

"I don't think so," I offer.

I'm kinder than he deserves.

"C'mon," he urges. "It's late. What else are you gonna do?"

He's trying to be playful, but it just makes me feel pathetic. I swell with a breath.

"I'm going out," I say. "With Miles."

"Who?"

I nod to where he's standing, talking to some folks at a table a few feet away, in his Mr. Rogers sweater and a pair of sparkly reindeer antlers that someone has put on his head. Nate glances from me to him and back again.

"You've got to be kidding me," he laughs. "Our neighbor?"

"My neighbor," I clarify.

I sense it swimming beneath his stare: jealousy. I hate to admit it gives me some level of satisfaction.

"How long's that been going on?"

I smile at the insinuation in his tone. I'll let him think it, if it gets under his skin.

"No," I say. "You don't get to act like this is why you left."

"I wasn't acting like that."

"Oh no?"

"No," he shrugs. "Just that you should be careful. You know none of these things with him last."

Heat prickles across my face, and in the dim mood lighting I wonder if he can see my cheeks turning red. I take a sip of what's left of my drink, hoping to hide it.

"Like that thing with you?" I say.

His face is impassive, but I can tell the hit has landed by the tiny, imperceptible twitch in his right eye. He nods, giving me a once over.

"Don't say I didn't warn you," he says, running a hand across my knee. "Night, Ceil."

All those good vibes I was riding high on have crash landed. I'm back where I started, wondering why anyone enjoys the holidays. Underneath all that glowing, happy exterior, there is an ugly emptiness, too. The fact that the world is filled with more have-nots than haves, and that all this excess is just a show. There's an expectation of magic and cheerfulness that is impossible for any single day to live up to. It's depressing.

By the time Miles slides onto the stool beside me, I'm considering that I might actually walk home. I want a reason for how numb I feel, and that bitter cold might do the trick.

"You ready to head out soon?" he asks.

"I think I might stay a while," I offer vaguely.

His gaze travels across my expression like he's reading the words plainly on my face. He nods, grabs a club soda, and saunters off. I roll my eyes, wondering if it was really that easy to get rid of him, but I realize as the place continues to clear out that he doesn't go. He helps his band pack up. He chats with some guys near the front windows, which are still frosty and dark and not at all hinting at anything half as magical as snow. He seems perfectly content to wait. For some reason, that annoys me.

Ari is wiping down the bar.

"Last call," she tells me. "We're closing up early. I hear that weather's moving in."

"Wishful thinking," I say. "Just my check?"

"He already got you."

I furrow my brow.

"Miles?" I ask.

I'm ready to berate him, as if this is proof that all of his actions tonight have been because he thinks I am a damsel in distress who can't take care of herself, just another girl he can bamboozle into his bed. I want to shout him down, tell him I'm not in need of rescuing, and march out of here in a blaze of self-sufficient glory.

"No," she says, looking a little confused. "Nate. That guy from earlier?"

I sink my head into my hands with a groan.

Notes drift up from the piano, and I don't have to turn to know that Miles has settled back onto the bench in front of it. It's that same warm-up melody I've heard a hundred times, but it transitions into something else. Something even more familiar. A song my dad used to play for me on an old 45. My namesake, and briefly during my adolescence, the bane of my existence. Miles's voice comes on strong.

"'Cilia,

You're breakin' my heart.

You're shakin' my confidence daily."

I swivel around so I can shoot him a look. He's smirking in my direction, leaning into that imaginary microphone and letting his hair fall into face. I swear he only does it so he has an excuse to toss it away.

"Oh Cecilia,

I'm down on my knees.

I'm begging you please to come home.

Come on home."

"You can stop anytime now," I call across the room.

The handful of patrons left at that front table laugh uncertainly. I turn back around. Ari shrugs an eyebrow at me.

"You should take him up on that ride," she says. "It's seriously cold out there."

"How do you even know about that?"

"I'm the bartender," she says with a sweep of her hand. "I see all."

I laugh a little, running my finger around the rim of my empty glass, while Miles carries on with the song. I've decided I'm ignoring him. It seems like the fastest way to get him to stop.

"What's the hesitation?" she says.

"It's... Miles," I offer. "I mean, he's just your everyday opportunistic heartbreaker. You know what I'm talking about."

"I do?" she asks, leaning her elbows on the bar, very interested now.

"Yeah, you know," I say, treading more carefully now in hopes I don't offend her. "You and him... You know I'm his neighbor. I see things, too."

"Oh," she laughs. "You mean the weekend I stayed there?"

She says it so casually I'm taken aback for a second.

"Yeah."

"I was just going through a tough time. My sister had just gone back to rehab, and I was trying to cover everything on my own, and I ended up losing my apartment. He let me crash on his couch until I could find a cheaper place. It was only a few days, but it kept me from sleeping in my car."

I blinked, stunned.

"Oh. I'm sorry, I just thought..."

"That we were sleeping together?" she asked, scrunching up her nose.

"Yeah," I admitted, feeling especially foolish.

"Maybe he's sleeping with someone," she laughed. "But it wasn't ever me. He's a good guy."

I realize absently that he's just singing the chorus over and over. When I turn around again, he's giving me that signature smirk. The fact that he even has a signature smirk should make me skeptical. For some reason, I find myself wearing a hint of a smile.

"I don't know any of the other words," he admits.

His playing slows to a stop, and he shrugs into his dark wool coat that looks like something sailors wear. I bet it has anchors on the buttons, and it feels so cliché, but it looks good on him. He pops the collar and smiles, tossing his head towards the door.

"You coming?"

9.

SOMETIMES IN LIFE YOU ENCOUNTER THOSE MOMENTS that give you a crisis of faith, times when all those things you have held to be right and true, the facts by which you navigate your world, are suddenly exposed to be very different than you imagined.

As a kid, it had been the night I fought sleep and peeked through the crack in the accordian doors leading into our den to find gifts being placed under the tree – not by Santa, with a red velvet sack, but by my parents, unloading items from an oversized Hefty bag. They were passing a glass of milk between them, and my dad had one of the cookies Eleanor and I had baked earlier that evening clutched between his teeth.

Suddenly, I was thinking about all those times he'd encouraged us to pick out Snickernoodle at the grocery store, because he had it on good authority that "those are the reindeer's favorite", and my seven-year-old heart stung with betrayal, because I felt like I should've known all along. It's the same way I felt about Nate, and about finding myself in the 1% failure rate for hormonal contraceptives only to be thrown into a sea of grief-stricken "why" a few weeks later, when I'd only just adjusted to the idea of being on the mothership in the first place.

Maybe it sounds insignificant, comparatively, but as I watch from the passenger seat as Miles uses a credit card to scrape the thin layer of frost off of his windshield, I feel equally as dumbstruck.

"Maybe he's sleeping with someone," Ari laughed.

He had definitely slept with someone. A few someones. That unmistakable soundtrack isn't up for debate. But how often have I heard it, really? Certainly not as often as I've seen girls leave his place. I hadn't heard it that night after the party, and I never kept that lunch date with Jenna, because I'm a sore loser, so I don't have any details about what actually went on between them. For all I know she air kissed everyone. And I had misread the situation with Ari. How many others have I gotten wrong? Is he running a Good Guy Crash Pad Hostel over there? If so, do I think that's more or less weird than his being a promiscuous jerk?

The truth is I still don't want to go home.

I don't know where I do want to go, though. I also don't know if there is anywhere else to go, unless you count that supposed speakeasy, which I do not. I wish I could fall out of time, into a place that is nowhere and everywhere, now and never. I consider maybe Miles's SUV is a close second. The windshield fogs over where he cleared it, and we're enveloped inside as we idle on the curb, waiting for the air coming out of the vents to go from frigid to warm. In this moment, we could be going nowhere and anywhere. It feels philosophical, almost. I might be a little drunk.

I chew the inside of my lip, watching as the lights of Matilda's go out. I hear myself sigh before I register that I'm doing it. The heat is almost lukewarm when he puts the truck in gear.

"You wanna go somewhere?" he asks.

I glance over, wondering not for the first time if he can read minds. It occurs to me that maybe he can just read me. I wonder what else is written all over my face.

"Care to be more specific?" I say. "Everywhere's closed."

"This isn't the kind of place that can be closed."

The green analog numbers on the dash read 10:34pm. I wonder why it feels like midnight, while simultaneously acknowledging that I feel hours from getting to sleep. I want to ask more questions, but honestly, I don't care where we're headed. It's been that kind of night.

"Am I dressed appropriately for this place that can't be closed?"

"If I say no, will it change your mind?"

I cut him a look.

"I'm kidding. You look great," he says.

The words tingle up my arms and along my collarbones, even though I know he didn't mean it like that. I look out the window again, watching as we transition from our cozy, eclectic neighborhood, past the bug-zapper glow of a twenty-four hour gas station, the multi-colored light display blinking outside the Children's Museum, and the desolate street-light orange of the fairgrounds. We cruise up the empty four lanes of one of the city's many oak-lined streets, and I notice the towering trees haven't even lost all of their leaves yet. Patches of brown and gold cling to their long-stretching arms, even in front of the house where we're turning in. Like many in this part of town, it has tall stone columns and wreaths on every warmly lit window. Unlike the rest, though, it also has a dozen cars in the driveway. Miles cuts the engine.

I'm not sure what I had imagined. Another bar, maybe, or that hot wing joint across town where Bearded Vest Guy was headed. I look over at him expectantly, but he's already getting out of the car.

"What is this?" I ask.

"It's a holiday tradition."

"That doesn't really answer my question."

I'm trailing after him anyway. The dark green front door has one of those knockers on it that looks like it belongs in the intro of an old MGM movie. Instead of reaching for it, his hand is on the doorknob, letting us inside. The smell of something warm and buttery hits me.

"We can't just walk into someone's house unannounced," I hiss.

He's laughing while he takes off his coat. As I'm arguing with him, my gaze settles down the long entryway, where I catch the edge of the most incongruous scene I've ever encountered. Are those... popcorn strands, stretched in sweeping arcs across the ceiling? It's hard to tell for all the cutout snowflakes, and the many strands of multi-colored string lights.

A woman sweeps around the corner in a retro tulle skirt and the most fabulous heels I've ever seen.

"Hey there, sweet boy! You made it!" she beams. "You're just in time for the merengue!"

She swishes her skirt for emphasis and kisses him like a mother, leaving a lipstick smudge on his cheek before wiping it off with her thumb. Motioning to me she asks, "And who is this lovely angel?"

In my shock, I realize Miles's hands are on my shoulders, helping me out of my jacket and scarf. If this woman is any indication, we are entirely underdressed for this party. She is smiling like she hasn't noticed.

"I'm Cecilia," I offer, shaking her hand.

"Welcome, Cecilia," she says, holding my hand in both of hers for a moment.

"This is Ms. Liv," Miles offers.

"Liv," she insists. "Olivia, even, if you want to feel proper. I haven't been able to break him from the prefix yet."

"Old habits," he smiles.

To me she says, "Well, darling, do you dance?"

"I, uh… sure sometimes."

She pats my arm, grinning slyly.

"Tonight you dance. It's tradition!" she says with a wink.

"Mom, I think something's burning," a guy calls, popping his head around the door. He's wearing jeans and the ugliest Christmas sweater I've ever seen. It's embroidered with the name Daniel. The stitching is a bit uneven, there are sparkles hanging from the collar, and the cuff of one sleeve looks like it's been gnawed on by a very angry dog.

"The poptarts!" Liv half-yells. "Excuse me!"

Miles laughs as she jets down the hall, her steps almost comically short in those magnificent heels.

"Sweet boy?" I ask him, raising an eyebrow.

"Ms. Liv's holiday tradition is limoncello, in case you hadn't noticed," he smiles.

I'm smiling too, though, I have no idea why. Confusion, perhaps, or maybe a little intrigue. The guy in the Daniel sweater is approaching us now, giving Miles an elaborate handshake.

"Hey, man. It's good to see you," the kid grins.

"You, too," Miles nods. "How was that first semester at State?"

"Man," the kid says, pulling a hand over his face. "Statistics kicked my ass."

"Maybe if you weren't minoring in Bud Light, you would've had a better chance," Miles jokes, motioning to the koozie-clad bottle in his hand.

"Dude, are you kidding me? We're nowhere close to affording Bud Light. More like Keystone."

His name, I learn in the next set of introductions, is not Daniel. It's Liam.

"They didn't have any Liam sweaters at Park Avenue Thrift," he shrugs.

Another dark-haired guy pops his head around the corner. His sweater has a big C stitched into the front. I'm not sure whether I believe it's an initial or another thrift store find.

"Yo, what are you guys doing? Merengue!"

Miles and Liam laugh, and suddenly we're moving towards the living room.

"What's a merengue?" I ask.

"You'll see," he smirks.

Latin music and laughter grow louder until we're surrounded by... whatever this is. The room is filled with those same haphazard strings of garland and multi-colored lights, giving the vaulted ceiling a glittery glow. The room is a swirl of formalwear, ugly sweaters, NBA jerseys, pajamas, and everything in between. One of the guys brushing past me is wearing a few links of chain around his neck, hanging full of tinkling bells. Half of everyone is a happy sort of drunk. The rest are well on their way there.

Liv is sweeping back into the room now, adding a platter of poptarts to the overflowing table of mismatched foods.

Miles grabs my hand and leads me into the fray. Suddenly, for the second time tonight, I'm dancing. People around us are smiling and shuffling to the beat. Old people, young people, even a woman holding a little terrier dog in a blue and white sweater, and I laugh. I have no idea what I'm doing. Miles must realize this, because he grins and motions to the way he's moving his feet. He slides a hand along the curve of my waist, pulling me into the rhythm and mimicking the movements of all the other couples.

Well, maybe not *all* the couples. There is a particularly saucy set near a big, scary, lifelike statue of Santa Claus, whose hands are roving each other in a way that makes me wonder how they still have their clothes on. They are being cheered on by everyone else.

"Is there a trick to this?" I ask over the revelry.

He leans in close to my ear, and his laugh is an exhale that tingles down my neck.

"You can't overthink it. You've just got to feel it."

I think about what I feel: the pulse of the beat, the gentle pressure of his hands on my hips, the way I can't stop smiling. There's a sway to this moment, a pull, like it's got its own gravity, and all I have to do is follow his lead. The rhythm is seductive. I close my eyes, allowing myself to melt with his movements. I'm entirely too Anglo-Saxon to be good at this, and maybe I look ridiculous, but I like the way it feels: all electric energy and body heat. When I open my eyes again, Miles is giving me that same, heart-tugging look that always drives me crazy.

He twirls me into a spin that nearly sends me into the couple behind us, and I'm laughing as he catches me against his chest. If anything I ever learned from Shakira is true, I have to stop this before my hips go telling him truths I can't take back. Like that the way he's watching me makes me feel impossibly sexy, and the way his hands are on me makes me very aware of my skin and what it would feel like for his fingers to smooth their way across it.

The song fades to another, equally as fast-paced beat, and I keep hold of his hand as I move away.

"I'm gonna find a drink," I say.

His fingers snag around mine until we're clear of the makeshift dance floor. I suck down bottled water like I just finished a spin class.

"You okay?" he asks.

"I dunno. I didn't know you were bringing me here for Christmas cardio."

There's a teasing in my voice, and I hope it will serve to bring me back from the bout of temporary insanity I'd experienced while butchering the merengue. There's still a flicker of wanting in my veins, and I decide it isn't him: it's probably just that I'm in the middle of a six-month drought and, hormonally speaking, I'm a little desperate for rain. Though that hadn't mattered much with Bearded Vest Guy, or Dancing Santa. I try not to think about it.

"Hey," he defends. "It's heart healthy."

He has grabbed a plate. Even though Hanukkah ended a few days ago, there's a menorah sitting on the bar and latkes piled on a tray beside a spiral cut honeybaked ham. There is also an array of crackers, dips, casseroles, and desserts. He has bypassed them all in favor of piling his plate high with what look to be tamales. He's already peeling open one of the corn husks when he catches me smiling at him.

"What?" he questions.

"What *is* this?" I laugh, looking around again.

He adds some poptarts to his plate before tossing his head towards the dining room. A raucous game of Trivial Pursuit is going on in here, and he says hi to a few people as we weave our way through, ending up in the cool air of a sunporch, that's only been made inhabitable by one of those tall outdoor heaters. It feels great, though, compared to the sultry sweat of the dance area. Miles sinks to a wicker couch and nods for me to do the same. I'm still watching him with a questioning gaze as he passes me one of the tamales.

"Ms. Liv's grandmother is Venezuelan," Miles explains. "She's ninety-eight-years-old, but she can wrap up a tamale in like five seconds flat. It's insane."

I take a bite, letting the flavors fill my mouth. It's like heaven: doughy, pork-filled heaven. I finish it before I realize, and he's passing me another.

"Miles," I finally say.

"Cecilia," he returns, equally as serious.

"What is this?"

"I told you already. It's a holiday tradition."

"Yes, but which holiday?"

"Yours. Mine. All of them."

I must be giving him a dubious look, because he finally puts down his plate and takes a drink.

"Okay, so this is the Dennisons' annual thing. It started way way back, probably before Andrew or his brothers were even born. Or at least before I started hanging around.

"Anyway, when she got married, Ms. Liv was really worried about losing the traditions she'd had as a kid. Like the tamales. And the merengue. They were being blended with the stuff Mr. Flynn's family celebrated, and she knew Andrew and the boys were going to pick up their own stuff from their friends and school and wherever, and – I'm really bad at telling this. You should get her to explain it."

"No, I think I get it," I smile. "Keep going."

"So she decided she was going to make it a point to keep them all. They were going to have a Traditional Holiday. She wrote down all the things that really mattered to them, and every year she made sure to check off every one. Any time someone new joins the party, they have to write down one thing they can't have Christmas – or Hanukkah, or Solstice, or Krampusnacht, or Endless Online Shopping – without. Over the years it kind of turned into this giant thing. And here we are."

I nodded. This explained the latkes and the sweaters and the paper snowflake ceiling, somehow. I unwrapped another tamale.

"So what was your contribution? The one thing you can't do Christmas without?"

He picks up one of the poptarts from the edge of his plate.

"I was ten when I joined the party," he defended. "And my mom wasn't really into baking, so when I was a kid we always left poptarts for Santa. I guess because that's what we had on hand."

I smile, imagining this.

"What are you going to put in the jar?" he asks.

I think about the standard things, like decorating the tree with ornaments we made as kids and watching all those classic claymation Christmas movies, but none of those seem right. Finally I say, "French toast. My mom always makes it on Christmas morning."

Miles nods appreciatively.

I'm suddenly so nostalgic I can't stand it. I fish my phone from my pocket, wondering when I'm going to get another update from them. Wondering if I have a right to wonder, really, after everything. My messages are empty.

"Do you need to head home?" he asks, like I'm checking the time.

"No," I say. "Sorry. My... sister's having a baby."

"Like... having a baby in general or...?"

"Like, right now."

"Oh shit," he says. "Suffice to say we're probably having a way better time tonight than she is?"

I laugh with a nod. Somehow, this is the first time I've thought about it that it doesn't sting quite as much.

"Most definitely." I grab a bite of strawberry poptart. "So, Andrew. Was he the one with the big C on his sweater?"

"No, that's his brother Callum. And you met Liam. Andrew, uh... he died. Five years ago."

That faraway look is a brief thing, but I feel bad about bringing it up.

"I'm so sorry," I say. "What happened?"

"Heroin," he shrugs.

He is trying to play it casual, but for once I can read him: this was one of those things that left a big scar and never stopped hurting. One of life's big gaping Whys.

"I'm sorry," I say again.

"Yeah," he says, meeting my eyes now. "Me, too."

"What was he like?"

"Fun," he says, a smile quirking across his face. "He was the life of the party, always. We sort of went different ways after high school, but for a lot of years... we were more like family than friends. I had my own mom, my own house, but it felt like I grew up here. We had actually just reconnected. I'd just moved back to town, and I heard he was getting himself together. He seemed good. It's just bizarre sometimes when I remember he's gone."

He pauses with a swig of his drink.

"But yeah, before that, a lot of fun. We had our first beers out behind Ms. Liv's rosebushes. Threw up our first beers out behind Ms. Liv's rosebushes. And the thrift store sweater thing? That was all him. He was obsessed with everything secondhand. Said he thought people had too much shit. Which was really fortunate for me in middle school, because I never had all the cool shit."

"He sounds like a good guy."

"He definitely had his moments," he agrees.

"Don't we all," I muse.

He breaks the last poptart in half and shares it with me. He's watching me for a moment before his gaze goes wistful. "I certainly hope so."

Inside, the music has died down, and I catch glimpses of the Trivial Pursuit crew moving away from the table. Voices carry through the open door.

"Story time!" someone yells from inside.

Both the poptart and the foggy gaze disappear in an instant. Miles stands, extending a hand to me.

"What's happening now?" I ask.

He grins.

"Haven't you caught on by now? It's tradition."

10.

THE LIVING ROOM HAS TRANSFORMED FROM A DANCE FLOOR to a seating area, and we crowd into the edge of the room. The entire party has migrated here. People are perched on chairs and couches and oversized pillows on the rug. Miles gives me a knowing smile as we lean against the doorframe, which offers us a clear view of tonight's next spectacle.

Standing by the life-size Santa is a tall man wearing a silk, Victorian nightcap and pretending to smoke an unlit cigar. He has the same sandy-colored hair as Liam, and I deduce by the way that Ms. Liv is looking at him adoringly that this is Mr. Flynn. He pulls a book off the edge of the fireplace and opens it with a flourish. A few loose note pages flutter out, and he collects them with a chuckle. With the papers tucked neatly into the book, he straightens up and starts again.

"'Twas a few days before Christmas," he begins.

A quiet laugh spreads through the room. I bite into my smile, rubbing my arms against the way chills have traveled up them. In this moment, we have all been changed from vivacious party-goers into children waiting for Santa. It's another one of those things I can't really explain, but it feels nostalgic and familiar, even though this evening is far from conventional. The story follows suit.

"'Twas a few days before Christmas,
When all through the house,
All our best friends were gathered
To good times espouse.
With dancing and drinking and fine things to wear,
In hopes that this holiday to none shall compare.
Guests gathered under snowflakes and popcorn on threads,
While Liv's limoncello shots buzzed in their heads."

A few people cheer at this point and raise their glasses.

"And Liv in her tulle skirt, and I in my cap,
Have no time or patience for a long winter's nap.
We've taken this season into our stead,
In hopes that the holidays no friend will dread."

I lean closer into Miles as someone nudges past us, and I catch his eyes for a moment as he smiles. I've never seen him so at ease. He's handsome. Not just cute, or smirky, or incredibly annoying, but handsome. That darkening hair and those blue eyes and that knowing upturn at the edge of his mouth, like he's in on a joke you just haven't figured out yet. Except this time it is different, like the joke is just between the two of us.

"Now poptarts! Now paper crowns! Now hard fruity seltzers!
On Bingo! On baklava! On ugly thrift store sweaters!"

As the listeners guffaw, I notice that Flynn Dennison is wearing one, too. It looks especially itchy and is embroidered with what are probably supposed to be reindeer but could also be rhinoceroses or giraffes. The life-size Santa is also wearing one. It's red and threadbare, and somehow I know if I was closer the four-letter pocket design would read Andy or Drew. Maybe in another setting this would seem weird, but I guess that's the thing about grief: some of us tuck it away and others invite it to their parties.

Flynn's booming voice grows theatrically quiet.

"When the evening had ended, when the dances were done,
When the guests were all worn out on good food and fun,
They sprang to their Rydes, to their friends blew a kiss,
And away they all went, their hearts filled with bliss.
But I heard them exclaim, as they drove out of sight--
Happy holidays to all..."

"And to all a good night!" the crowd replies.

Applause engulfs the room as Flynn snaps the book shut and takes a bow so low that the nightcap slides off his head. One of the boys grabs it and attempts a quick getaway, dodging around the guests who are shuffling to their feet. There is a flurry of commotion as everyone moves to refill plates and beverages.

"Is that it?" I ask.

"In case you haven't figured it out yet," Miles says, "this is one of those infomercial evenings."

"Infomercial evenings?"

"But wait, there's more."

I lean into him with a laugh, because there is indeed more. Liv has already produced a fresh bottle of limoncello and is sashaying her way behind the bar, ready to serve up another round. I'm considering it when an older gentleman nearby clinks his spoon against his glass, and the *ting-ting-ting* fills the air. A gentle hush falls over the room. A few others join in. It reminds me of weddings, when everyone summons the bride and groom together for a kiss. I imagine they're doing it for our hosts, but then I realize the man is looking at me. Or more specifically, *us.*

My face floods with instant-match-light heat as I glance at Miles. I can feel it lurking above us before I follow his gaze up, the way you can sense a giant palmetto bug on the wall behind you, or a bad haircut before the stylist swivels you around to face the mirror, or any other sort of impending doom. I don't know for sure, but I have a feeling that the leafy green ball hanging above us is mistletoe. I'm surprised anyone spotted it amidst the tangle of sparkly silver garland and snowflakes and string lights, but there it is.

The tinkling of glassware is growing by the second, and my pulse begins galloping in my chest like a fledgling deer. My mind is shuffling through options. I could run from the room and tear out of the house, which wouldn't be at all mood-killing or dramatic. I could kiss him, which given this room full of spectators feels a little too much like being thirteen with braces in a game of spin-the-bottle. Or I could continue to stand here like an idiot, which is the option that's winning out.

Miles is giving me one of those stares that tugs straight through my center, and if ever there is a time I want him to read my thoughts it's now. His mouth is a flicker of a smile. He takes my hand and, with a courtly little bow, presses his lips against my knuckles.

The clinking gives way to a collective "aww" and appreciative applause. Everyone is suddenly shuffling around us again, preoccupied with tarts and tamales. I smile as our fingers slip apart.

"I could almost kiss you for that," I say.

"Wouldn't be the first time," he smirks.

My face warms again, and I laugh. Partly because he's such a cocky bastard. And partly because he's right.

***

About that.

I haven't even told Joss about that.

It's not that I meant to keep it a secret as much as I was hoping I could trick myself into believing it didn't happen at all. For the most part that tactic has worked, helped along by one very pungent cup of Witch's Brew, which is the only thing that our mutual friend Tavian was serving at his "Dirty Thirty"

Costume Ball. I'm not getting drunk at parties half as often as it might seem, but apparently when I do, it's a law of the universe that Miles is bound to saunter in. I guess some might call that fate; I call it a recurring inconvenience.

From the rooftop of Tavian's downtown apartment, I could see the whole city stretched out beneath me, all the way into the dark trees to the east and the bridge that headed in from the west, which was casting the purple glow of its evening lights along the wide expanse of the river. The full moon was a perfect, hazy orb in the sky, looking every bit the sort that would summon werewolves and mayhem of all kinds. I had started the evening taking portraits of the birthday gent in his Goblin King ensemble and had eventually devolved into capturing the group festivities, which now had lured me to a quiet spot near some overgrown topiaries, where I had a perfect view of the sky. I studied the shot I had just taken and adjusted my settings.

Just a few more, I told myself, and I'd rejoin the party.

One of the things I love about being a photographer is how it can pull you into the center of everything. Some people pose, some people scoff, but when you raise that lens they usually notice you, regardless. They smile and invite you in, hoping you'll snag a piece of this moment and make it a memory. But being behind the camera can also have the opposite effect. There were times I felt removed from everything, in the moment only as an observer, and in those moments I seemed to become invisible. Sometimes that feeling frustrated me, but on this particular night, it was like ducking into the shadows of my own little world, where I blended in especially well with my black-on-black outfit, which I'd adorned with cat ears and some hastily drawn whiskers for the occasion.

For a few savory moments, it was just me, with the last warm breezes of the year on my skin, and this beautiful, endless sky, with its 3D horror-movie clouds and its bright Hunter's Moon bathing everything in silver.

"What are you supposed to be: bad luck?"

I knew it was him before I turned, and I lifted my camera and snapped his picture. People hate when you do that.

He was wearing a gold vest and a black waistcoat, which he adjusted casually, as if he didn't mind.

"You know this is a costume party, right?" I said. "You're supposed to come as something other than the everyday asshole that you are."

"All you did was put on cat ears," he defended. "I, at least, added a cravat."

I exhaled a laugh, wondering if I'd ever heard anyone use the word 'cravat' in real life before. He eased to the railing beside me, watching as I pulled my viewfinder back out towards the water.

"Who are you supposed to be, anyway?"

"Beethoven," he said. "Or Mozart. Or Bach. Really just whichever one people recognize. I wear this sometimes for class. Except there's a wig. The kids love it."

"But the ladies not so much?"

I'd seen him waltz in alone, though he'd almost immediately been accosted by a Sexy Police Officer, whose skirt was one attempt at sitting down away from becoming a crime of indecency. She reminded me of the neonatal nurse, and both of them were shorter and blonder than me. I figured he had a type.

He dragged a hand through his hair, sweeping it to the side.

"You'd still think I was hot in a wig," he offered.

"When have I ever said you were hot?"

"You didn't have to say it."

I glanced at the grid of city lights beneath us, hoping to prevent him from any other revelations, like realizing he was right. I snapped a picture of the streetlight glow.

"Remember when we said no flirting?" I asked.

"That was a long time ago."

"Is there a statute of limitations?" I laughed.

"I think so. I mean, you said you'd get back to me."

I stilled under his gaze, feeling the heat spread under my skin. There were broad strokes of that night, and then there was that, which was wrapped up with his hand in my hair and my breath against his mouth. I'd always assumed it hadn't meant anything to him. He was a little drunk, and he'd been onto the next convenient thing as soon as I went to bed, so why did he care to remember that?

"I did say that," I agreed.

"That's a long time to keep a guy waiting."

"You seemed to be plenty preoccupied without me."

There was a shift in his expression, but I couldn't read it.

"As did you," he offered.

With the way he was looking at me, it's no wonder girls were always following him home. It's a look that taunted and toyed and tugged until we were standing shoulder to shoulder, with me turned out towards the cityscape and him facing in towards the topiaries edging the party. My pulse simmered beneath my skin.

"We also said no touching," I said, glancing at the point where his arm leaned against mine. "In case you forgot."

"I didn't forget."

His smirk was a devilish thing. He leaned in confidentially, bringing his words in close to my ear. "And I don't have to touch you to make you want me."

I knew it was just a line, but chills spread down my neck anyway. I closed my eyes for a moment, but it only exacerbated the feeling that the closer he got, the closer I wanted him to be.

"Where did we land on kissing?" he asked.

His words were a whisper that tickled along my ear. Every nerve in my body was responding to all those ways he wasn't touching me. His gaze was trailing those imaginary kisses down my neck, along my jaw, across the curve of my mouth.

My sigh fell across his lips, which were now so close I could feel the sliver of space between us like it was a tangible thing.

"We didn't," I breathed.

Now it was his turn to sigh. His breath became the brush of his lips. He grazed his mouth against mine like he was testing, teasing, and this not-quite-kiss was everything. It was the heat in my veins and this insatiable feeling of wanting him.

I sank into it.

He released a subtle groan as I leaned in, catching my mouth against that sound that was half-surprise, half-relief. It consumed me. The way his fingers crept up my spine, how he teased his tongue along my bottom lip, then the top, drawing me deeper. Wanting pooled deep in my center. A soft little sigh escaped me.

He was too damn good at this.

We traded kisses, slow, hungry, aching. His hands were in my hair, and mine were sliding inside his coat, and my stomach flipped like the ground was coming up fast beneath me.

What the hell was I doing?

I sucked in a breath, pulling back. My lips felt clumsy and swollen, bitten by the sudden cold.

"I'm sorry," I said, running my hands through my hair. "I can't..."

"Sorry," he breathed. "Did I...?"

"No. I dunno," I admitted.

I wasn't ready for this. I wasn't ready to become one of his one-night stands. I wasn't ready to awkwardly avoid him when we crossed paths, or to set myself up to get my heart broken again. I just needed him to be my neighbor, and we'd only just gotten good at that. I needed this to not be complicated.

"This," I said. "This never happened, okay?"

I couldn't read that expression either, but I knew that smirk. He nodded, pulling himself off the rail and straightening his jacket. He was already moving away.

"Your whiskers are smudged."

I leaned against the cool metal and bit into the feel of his lips against mine, as I stared at the cars rolling along those grid-line streets. I didn't stick around to see if he took Sexy Police Officer home, but I heard him come in around one. That piano music started up, and I wondered if he was playing it for her, or himself, or... me.

11.

 that looks like a goblet meant for Tinkerbell, and Callum lobs a snowball right at Miles's face. He dodges it at the last second, only to have it smack a scandalized-looking woman in the arm. She picks it up, looking at it curiously, before her mouth twitches into a tiny grin.

"Oh," she nods. "It is -- what do you boys call it -- on?"

Their faces flash surprise as she downs her drink and launches it back.

"Snowball fight!" Callum bellows.

Of course, it's not really snowing. Not a flake, nor a flurry, or even the more-common-around-these-parts freezing rain. That doesn't stop the brothers Dennison from sending glittery-white balls of hard-pressed foam and felt flying through the air. This is apparently one of those things that Flynn Dennison, having grown up in Pennsylvania, can't do Christmas without. There must be a hundred of them, and the room descends into giggles and chaos. Miles arms himself with half a dozen and drags me behind the Christmas tree.

"What's the object of this?" I ask as he passes me one.

"Hit or be hit."

I dodge an incoming attack.

"Until what?"

"Until we all surrender."

I have no idea why I'm laughing. Callum and Liam are clearly favorite targets. The littlest kids have taken to standing directly by the large crate of ammo and pummeling them over and over. Others take a more strategic approach, seeking out spouses and parents and coworkers. Liv, who seems to be impervious to the entire thing, is laughing unscathed with a drink in one hand and a poptart in the other. Miles and I are hemmed in, however, because of all the people trying to take out Callum and Liam, they are only trying to take out us.

My first shot goes flying wildly into the abyss of a hallway.

"You have to aim," Miles says.

"I was aiming."

"For what?" he laughs.

I throw the ball in my hand against his chest. He levels a stare at me that is clearly a challenge.

"Oh, you're gonna regret that."

I shriek and leap from behind the tree as he launches a series of snowballs at me. I'm collecting an armful as I scurry across the room, ducking behind the sofa and throwing them wildly in his direction. Some of them land, most do not, but he is laughing so hard that his forward motion is stalled, helped in large part by the Dennison clan's mission to take him down. As much as I enjoy everyone ganging up on him, I feel it my duty to balance the odds, and I begin an attack against the brothers once again. Miles uses this as an opportunity to join me behind the sofa.

"Are you a double agent now?" he asks.

"You act like I have a plan," I reply, ducking from a near hit.

He catches a snowball to the cheek when he pops up a little

too high. His smile is shimmery, and so is his hair, and I wonder if we're going to leave here looking like we just emerged from a Spice Girls concert.

"What? Cecilia doesn't have a plan? Or rules? That's a first."

I smack him with another glitter bomb just for good measure. He picks it up and launches it over the couch.

"I think we've got them on the ropes!"

I can't tell if he's right, but after a few more minutes of rapid-fire chaos, Callum calls a truce, and we all collapse to the floor with our hearts pounding and chests heaving. Christmas cardio, indeed.

I'm lying on the area rug, staring up at the sparkly light-up ceiling, wondering at how I haven't felt this much like a kid, well, since I was actually a kid. It reminds me of the time Ellie and I moved all the gifts so we could sleep under the tree.

"Was that the last of the traditions?" I ask.

"Oh no. We're going to be washing glitter off of us for days. It's the gift that keeps on giving," he laughs. "And I already told you, there's more."

"What *more* can there possibly be?"

"What happened to 'young and spontaneous'?" he teases. "I guess next time I can print you up an itinerary, if that'll make you feel better."

"Next time."

I know it was a turn of phrase, but I like the way color creeps across his cheeks anyway. He pulls me to my feet, and we grab a couple of latkes before he ushers me outside, where sparklers sizzle across the yard.

"The grand finale," he explains.

Just like at weddings, the long sticks are arranged in a big glass jar. He grabs a few and lights one. It sizzles to life, shooting sparks out into the dark. He offers me one, and I hold it tentatively as he lights it with his. I swirl it around, watching the way the light trails. Across the yard, a few kids are doing the same, dancing like fairies through the cold. As if to offer appropriate juxtaposition, Liam occupies the other corner, using his empty beer bottles to launch the aptly named bottle rockets. They whistle and pop as they shoot into the sky. A few of his friends laugh.

"Fireworks are the final tradition?"

"It's really more for the song. We all get together and sing 'White Christmas'," he explains. "Or, um, 'Bright Christmas', as it were'."

"This night has more singing and dancing than a musical."

"Are you not entertained?"

His teasing tone flutters through me. I'm already laughing as he brandishes his sparkler like a sword, swishing it towards mine, when someone yells, "Watch out!"

It happens in a slow-motion instant. Our smiles falter, replaced by quick-spreading panic. We're dropping our makeshift swords, and Miles is wrapping himself around me, and I am folding into him. Our sparklers fizzle to smoke in the grass as the rogue rocket pops off. He holds me against his chest for a second more, and there's a warm safety in this closeness, intertwined with the soft, intoxicating smell of him. I feel his words thrum through his chest where I've buried my face.

"Dude," he calls across the yard.

It's a warning that makes him sound for once like a teacher, and Liam appropriately replies, "Sorry! Sorry."

We realize the threat has passed. Miles slips away from me now, running an awkward hand through the front of his hair. The cold takes his place.

"You okay?"

"Yeah," I nod.

"Sorry. I didn't mean to violate your 'no touching' rule."

He's halfway teasing, but my pulse still simmers.

"There's actually an addendum to the 'no touching' rule, in which you're more than welcome to save me from bodily harm."

That smirk creeps across his mouth again.

"Good to know."

He retrieves a couple of fresh sparklers, and we join the others who step outside to sing what turns out to only be the chorus of "White Christmas", over and over and over, before a series of small fireworks burst into the sky. The embers trail through the air like snow, and I think that 'bright' is much more likely than 'white', at least around here. I'm watching the last of them sparkle blue and gold.

"Are you about ready to head home?" he asks.

I'm not, really. Not at all. But I nod. Liv gives us both big hugs as we head for the door.

"You kids be good, okay?" she calls after us.

"No promises," Miles replies, and she laughs.

In the quiet of the car, I check my messages. There are two waiting: one from about half an hour ago, sent over by my mom, and a more recent one from Nate.

Hey sweetie, you awake? he has the nerve to ask.

I think it's going to be a long night, Mom reports.

I think, somehow, she's right.

12.

MY MOM HAS THIS TALENT OF IGNORING when anyone isn't getting along like it's a lifestyle choice. Maybe that's why she can send me updates about my sister's extended stay in Labor & Delivery like the Baby Shower Incident never happened, when the reality of the situation is that my status as an aunt in any capacity beyond the most basic and biological is up for debate.

I should begin by telling you, I've never enjoyed baby showers. Grown people who entertain themselves with trying to determine which chocolate candy has been smeared across a diaper kind of freak me out. Add that to the mocktails, the monochrome color schemes, and being forced to make small talk with a bunch of women you don't know and would never hang out with otherwise, and you've pretty much got my worst nightmare. Even in my planning-brain blip of being pregnant, I had never intended on having a shower, in the traditional sense. I should've said no.

"You can't say no," Eleanor had told me on the phone. "I know you've been busy, but this is our last chance to hang out before the baby."

Ah, guilt. The thing holding families together for centuries.

Her best friend's new construction in the suburbs where we grew up was brimming with ankle boots and layered sweaters when I arrived. These weren't my kind of girls. These were the kind of girls who had gone to college at big-name state schools and came out with their Mrs degrees, who introduced themselves to everyone as So-and-so's wife and Insert-retro-baby-name-here's mom, and conducted themselves in a way that made them seem at least ten years older than me. It's not that I was trying to be judgy, except that this lot was traditionally very judgy, and it always put me on edge, like every moment in a room with them was laced with the need to defend my identity.

Among all these modern neutrals, it was easy to spot Ellie, wearing a floor-length red dress and looking especially ripe, like some sort of melon, or gourd, or ancient fertility goddess. I deposited my gift – a cutesy set of bamboo crib sheets that I would not see her open – onto the blue and yellow gift wrap mountain and gave her a wave.

"Cee!" she squealed.

The hug she pulled me into was mostly belly, and afterwards she rubbed her hands over it like a crystal ball.

"Look at you," I offered. "You look --"

"Giant," she groaned. "Every time I think I can't get bigger, I do."

"Beautiful," I corrected.

"Oh, c'mon. Everyone just says stuff like that so I don't get hysterical," she laughed. "Have you met Jen?"

Before I could reply, Ellie was dragging our host out of another conversation by the elbow and making introductions.

"Oh, hiiii," Jen was saying, which was code for, *how sure am I that we don't already know each other?*

"We met," I offered with a polite smile.

"At the wedding," she agreed, though she still didn't seem

entirely sure. "So good to see you! So glad you could come all this way!"

"Yeah," I said. "It's not too far."

"Oh well, I guess it just seems far," she chortled. "Like a whole different world!"

"Definitely," I smiled.

Thank god, I thought.

"But please. Make yourself at home. And grab a plate! There's food, there's wine."

She said this last bit with a scandalous giggle, and Eleanor rolled her eyes.

"Jen has decided to get me back for all the times she had to play DD for me when she was pregnant with her first, by serving endless bottles of my favorite wine," she explained, "at my own baby shower, when she knows I cannot have any."

"Well, you're the only one complaining!" Jen laughed. "And you know, my doctor always said a glass of wine during the third trimester is perfectly safe."

"Oh no," another friend warned, edging into the conversation. "Are we really going to have this debate again?" To me she adds, "It always gets heated. Last time I thought there was going to be a slap-fight."

"Sounds festive," I said.

"Anyway, could you check on mom for me?" Ellie asked. "I think she's in the kitchen. She's been completely freaking out about this sash thing, I dunno. And people think I'm emotional."

"You should take her some wine," Jen suggested before sweeping off.

Nobody needed to tell me twice. I filled a couple of glasses with the fruity plum beverage that was right up Eleanor's alley – almost too sweet to drink, and probably about as alcoholic as a standard beer – and eased into the kitchen, where my mom was indeed having a minor breakdown over attaching glittery letters intended to spell Mom-To-Be across a white strip of silky fabric.

"You need help?" I asked.

"Oh, Cee," she sighed. "How's your stitching? I've already pricked myself about a dozen times, and I cannot for the life of me get this B to stay put. I should've known better. The adhesive that comes with these things never works."

"Too bad the baby's name isn't going to start with the letter E. Ya know? Then it would be like 'Mom-To-E'."

She cut me a look.

"Is it really that big of a deal?"

"I just want everything to be perfect."

I sighed and took the needle from her. Let the record show that I did this because, despite my own emotional baggage, I too wanted everything to be perfect. I managed to prick myself on the second stitch. I paused to grimace.

"See," Mom said, taking a self-satisfied sip of her drink. "It's not just me!"

After about fifteen minutes of stitching, arguing, and intermittent Googling, we got the sash draped around Ellie like a beauty queen and joined the others in the living room. With the crisis averted, we were left to mingle and await the dreaded "games". We've already covered how I feel about those, so I quickly started my own little game, which was Drink Anytime Anyone Says Something That Makes You Want to Stab Them in the Face.

"Didn't you get married?" a petite girl who resembled a Yorkshire Terrier asked.

Drink.

"Oh," I said. "No, I didn't."

"Oh! But you were engaged, right?"

"Sorry, no."

Drink.

"I think I'm confusing you with someone else," the Yorkie

laughed. "I thought you were Eleanor's sister."

Drink.

After five minutes of listening to this woman demonstrate how she was not the brightest bulb on the Christmas tree, I was grabbing a refill.

"No, not Ashlynn. You're thinking of Kylie," a young Kelly Ripa was saying as I sat back down.

"Didn't they just have their third?" her friend asked.

"*Why* would they be having a third?" the one with the orange spray tan chimed in. "Jeez, haven't they heard of birth control."

Drink.

"Oh no, didn't you hear they lost the baby?" Young Kelly Ripa said.

"Oh no, that's terrible," the first friend offered. Her tone was that of someone who found this news to actually be more disappointing than terrible.

"This is why you should never announce early. You know she had already posted all those ultrasound pictures?" young Kelly Ripa said. "Just so unfortunate."

Drink, drink.

"So, Cecilia, do you have any kids?"

Drink, drink, drink.

It's not that I thought drinking was the answer, it's just that I couldn't take any more of their stupid fucking questions. I had a third glass during the Guess That Baby Food game, if for no other reason than to wash the putrid taste of a brown paste that turned out to be Ham and Gravy out of my mouth, and poured a fourth as Ellie started opening gifts and we began Baby Shower Bingo, during which we were supposed to cross items off of our card as they were unwrapped. We had all been given blue markers for the task, and Ellie was perched in a big armchair by Jen's gloriously oversized tree, looking like a Christmas angel, even though the rogue B was already peeling off of her sash.

"But before we begin," Jen said, leaning against the arm of the chair, "a toast to our very sweet, very sober Eleanor as she prepares to finally join the club!"

Appreciative giggles tittered through the room before we all collectively took a drink.

"Ellie," she continued, "I'm just so happy for you to embark on this journey of motherhood. It's truly the most beautiful, most meaningful, most rewarding thing you will ever do, and we're all just so very happy for you!"

Most beautiful, most meaningful, most rewarding, I thought. As if the rest of us were just living ugly, meaningless, worthless existences. I was feeling every bit the bitter bitch, party of one, when I took another drink. My mom was beside me, dabbing at her eyes.

"Are you crying?" I asked.

She didn't respond, just cut me a look like she used to when we were little kids, acting up in church.

"Is this about the sash?"

"Oh hush," she said now, swatting at me with a sigh.

Maybe it's then I noticed my words were coming a little too easily and my thoughts felt a little too fluid, as if either of them could slip right through my filter at any point. I glanced into my glass. What the hell was in this wine?

As we suffered through the slow unveiling of every embroidered burp cloth, monogrammed onesie, and conflict-free diaper cream, it became even more apparent that maybe I had overdone it. My head was swimming a little, and I might have spilled a touch of plum wine on Jen's modern-neutral rug when I changed the cross of my legs. Eventually I meandered back to the refreshment table, at which point I discovered that despite tasting remarkably similar to the liquid from a jar of maraschino cherries, this shit I'd been downing was fifteen percent alcohol. Fifteen percent! I blinked at the label, already planning to switch to water, when I heard the collective *oohs* and *ahhs* move through the group.

I was expecting another tiny outfit or cutesy bottle brush, and then I saw it. Buzzed or not, I knew exactly what it was, even before my mom began to explain.

"Oh my god," I said.

I hadn't meant to say it out loud, but when the entire room turned to look at me, I knew it must've been. Loud.

Ellie was smiling at me now, holding Mr. Snugglebottom.

That button-eyed, velvet-covered bear that had belonged to my mother, and my grandmother, and possibly another generation before that. By the time we were kids, he had earned a spot on a high shelf, and we were only allowed to play with him on special occasions, but that didn't stop us from making up elaborate stories about him, to the point that he had always felt like a beloved member of the family. He had his own mythology. His own lore. Now, Ellie was holding him against her swollen belly, grinning from ear-to-ear.

"I know! Can you believe it?" she exclaimed.

"No," I said.

The force of it left everybody smiling nervously, like maybe I had meant it much more "no, haha" than it sounded. Ellie knew, though. Her cheeks were turning the same color as her dress, but she looked determined to make light of this and save face.

"C'mon, Cee," she laughed. "Don't be jealous that I get to play with him first."

Those nervous smiles around us turned to giggles, and all I could do was stare. I knew she didn't mean to stab me straight through, but she did. My face felt hot and tingly with emotions I couldn't even name. My plum-wine brain, however, summarized them succinctly as, "Oh fuck you."

"Cecilia," my mom gasped.

The ankle boot crew was gaping at me now. Ellie looked like

I had slapped her, and Jen was moving in quickly, like she was hoping to do damage control. It didn't help that I was holding a barely empty bottle of wine. She plucked it from my hand on her way past.

"Okay, let's just take that!" she quipped.

"Oh okay. Sure. Thanks."

My mom was glaring at me like an unruly teenager.

"Kitchen," she mouthed. "Now."

I could still hear Jen bringing out the next gift and trying to get things back on track in the other room as I folded my arms across my chest and leaned against the white cabinets. I imagined everyone was half-paying attention, half-wishing they could listen at the door to the conversation I'd just been dragged into.

"What on earth is the matter with you? Are you *drunk*?" Mom hissed. "Who gets drunk at a baby shower?"

"What the fuck was that, Mom? Mr. Snugglebottom?"

"You are making a scene!"

"You can't give her Mr. Snugglebottom," I said, more loudly now. "What if I was having a baby? Who would you give him to then?"

"Well, you're not having a baby, so I don't think that really matters right at this moment!"

My nose was stinging from the force of trying not to cry, like I'd sucked saltwater up it, when Eleanor popped into the room.

"We can still hear you," she said, her voice low and panicky. "What the hell is going on?"

"I was just asking Mom the same thing."

"Is this really... are you seriously trying to ruin this for me? Over a stupid bear?"

"Both of you, stop."

"No, really," she pressed. "Are you really that upset because I get something and you don't? This is my day. This is my baby shower."

On some level, yeah, my feelings were just as petty and childish as she thought. But underneath that, this was something else completely. It was heartbreak, and rage, and rejection, and every shade of humanity in between.

"I know this might come as a shock to you, Eleanor, but not everything is about you," I spat.

"Why can't you just be happy for me? Are you trying to embarrass me?"

"What do you want from me? You want me to treat you like all your idiot friends who act like you're the only person in the world to ever fucking procreate?"

"Oh, I dunno. Do you expect me to treat you like you're the only person who's ever been dumped before?"

"That is enough!" Mom hissed.

"Yes," I agreed. "Yes, it is."

My plan to stay the night at my parents' house across town, with them and Eleanor, was obviously out, so I called Joss to come drive me home. I sat in my car, where I'd parked it around the corner, with the seat back and the music up. When she showed up an hour and a half later, she looked pretty pissed at me too.

"That was a $250 Ryde," she said, taking my keys.

"Worth it," I replied.

She climbed into the driver's seat and turned us in the direction of home. Maybe it was my sister, maybe it was me, but regardless of who started it, we hadn't spoken since.

13.

Nate's message is burning a hole in my pocket. I want to type a furious reply and tell him what a fucking fraud he is. I also don't want to give him the satisfaction of a reply, even a nasty one. What business is it of his if I'm awake? Does he honestly think he's going to come over here and hang out like we're old friends? Why haven't I just blocked him already? This is seriously masochistic.

I think about it the whole way home, and when Miles cuts the engine in front of our shared sidewalk, I stare up at the single lamp glowing in my front window.

"You okay?" he asks.

"Have you ever hated someone?"

"Um."

"I mean, like honestly-wanna-stab-them-in-the-throat hated someone?"

I glance over, realizing most people would look at least a little nervous if the girl in the passenger seat launched herself into this rant, but he's actually considering it.

"I don't know about stab-them-in-the-throat hate, but I've definitely experienced the wanna-burn-all-their-shit-in-my-fire-pit fury," he says. "Which you're more than welcome to do, if you think that'll make you feel better. A little less messy than the stabbing."

I laugh in spite of myself. I have no idea what I'm doing, so much so that when he asks if I want to come in, I'm actually considering it. As much as I started this night willing to be anyone's one-night stand, I definitely don't want to be his, and we're historically not great at keeping our distance. I acknowledge, though, that we've made it this far into the evening without incident, even despite that faulty firework and poorly placed mistletoe.

"Maybe," I sigh. "As long as you understand I'm not interested in being your next breakup album."

He sinks against the steering wheel with a hopeless laugh. "Why do you always do that?"

"Do what?"

"Assume the worst of me."

I don't exactly know what to say to this, so I stall with a shrug.

"I'm just telling you how it looks," I offer.

"You care too much about how things look."

"I make my living caring too much about how things look."

"Well, could you change your lens? It's starting to give me a complex."

Despite the cocky glare he gives me before he climbs out into the cold, a few moments later he's opening my door.

"If you wanna go home, I totally understand. If, however, you want to come over and hang out with your half-as-much-of-an-asshole-as-you-seem-to-think-he-is neighbor, I promise not to con you out of your clothes or reenact any part of 'Baby, It's Cold Outside'," he says. "Although, it is fucking cold outside, so whatever choice you're gonna make, could you do it quickly?"

It's probably no surprise to anyone but me when I follow him up the walk.

His place smells like a library. A very homey, vanilla-citrus and cedar kind of library. And it's a helluva lot warmer than my place has been lately. The rest of it is mostly as I remember: filled with books and art and lamps and mismatched furniture. Major Tom is atop the piano, rousing himself from what looks to be a long winter's nap and stretching into a downward facing dog pose as we enter.

"You want something to drink?" he asks. "I've got water, maybe some wine."

"Very biblical of you," I say. "Just whatever."

He plugs in the lights of the three-foot Christmas tree lurking in the corner, and I realize this little touch is infinitely more festive than anything I've done in my apartment this season. His bar is lined with holiday cards, some of which look handmade by his middle school students, and underneath them he's hung two stockings. I smile, hoping one is for Tom.

"'Just whatever' it is," he announces.

He disappears into the kitchen, and I linger in the hallway, where the wall is an array of tour posters. Post-hardcore, punk, piano rock, a few random pop bands. I spot a colorful one for a summer festival and find The Devils & the Details lurking in the jumble of bands near the bottom. I'm smiling as he returns, passing me a glass of malbec.

"What's it like, being on tour with these guys?" I ask. "I mean, I'm pretty sure I was screaming along to some of these when I was sixteen and wearing way too much eyeliner."

"Same," he smirks.

I give him a sideways glance, to which he responds, "Hey, I look damn good in eyeliner."

We're laughing as we ease back into the living room, and he sinks across a nearby chair that's velvety and red.

"It's kind of bizarre, I guess. Sometimes I feel like a complete imposter, like we're gonna show up and they're going to tell us we're not on the list or something. But other times, it's, I dunno, pretty cool. Feels like a dream."

"You think you'd ever do it full-time?"

"Tour? No," he scoffs.

I lean against the edge of the piano, scratching Tom's chin. He puffs out his whiskers like a miniature tiger.

"Too much sex, drugs, and rock-and-roll?"

"Too much Taco Bell and cheap hotels," he counters. "We did it for a few years. It helped us get our name out there, and it's great for the summer, but I'm worried if I did it all the time I wouldn't love it anymore."

"Um, I happen to share a wall with you. I know that you are in fact doing this all time," I say, tapping my fingers along the nearest keys. The notes thrum through the room.

"Well, the music's different. I've always done that. Always will."

"Always always?"

"Since I was like seven or eight."

He shrugs like it's nothing. I'm impressed, but I perch on the edge of the bench and give him my own shrug.

"Most guys go for guitar."

He knows what I'm doing.

"I'm not most guys," he smirks. "I also didn't have a guitar. But I did have my grandfather's old piano and way too much time on my hands."

"At seven," I say incredulously.

"My mom worked a lot."

I understand this isn't something he wants to talk about.

"It worked out," I shrug.

"Most things do," he nods, taking a sip of his drink.

As cynical as I've been feeling, I appreciate the sentiment. I fill the next five seconds with the intro to "Fur Elise", clumsy and one-handed. That's all that remains of my childhood lessons, which were as short-lived as my ballet career, my time in youth league soccer, and my dad's hope I'd get really into tennis. I don't do the melody much justice, but when I spin back around he's smiling.

"You're not going home for Christmas this year?" he asks.

"Not this year," I admit. "My parents are staying with my sister, and things are a little... crowded."

"Oh yeah, how's the baby watch going?"

I check my phone with a shrug, deleting Nate's next lingering unread message in the process.

"Nothing yet."

Maybe there's a sigh in my voice. Maybe there's sadness in my tone. Maybe it's the resigned way I take a gulp of my malbec. Whatever the reason, I hear him saying, "I'm sorry. That has to be hard."

I'm watching him now, from across the room. I can't ever read him, but somehow when I look at him, I *know*. I know that he knows I'm not just not going home because of the close quarters and the long drive. He stills, and suddenly he knows that I know as well. The sound that escapes me is a humorless one. I set my glass on top of the piano.

"We *really* need thicker walls," I say bitterly.

Maybe he's agreeing, or apologizing again, but I can't hear him over the roaring thoughts in my head. I wonder how much he heard, but I know the answer to this. Everything. All those yelling arguments I had with Nate about being pregnant, and about not being pregnant, just as well as I know those stupid piano melodies and the rhythm of his bed. I am laid bare, and I hate it.

"So that's it?" I ask. "You invited me over because you feel sorry for me?"

"What? God, no."

I'm already moving for the door, and he's springing out of his chair. Even if he hadn't heard everything, he'd heard enough. Enough that I take back everything I said when I was sitting at the bar, because at this moment, all I want for Christmas is for him to have never been my neighbor.

"Cecilia," he says. "Can you just stop for one second?"

I grab my coat off the rack and sling open the front door. The cold rushes in, and it's a welcome sting, because I'm hot with shame and betrayal and anger. Then I stop in my tracks. I'm hugging my coat against my chest and gaping into the heavy wool sky.

He stops too. For a few moments, everything is so still and quiet. The streets are empty, the city is silent, and the indignant rage in my veins is replaced by hushed awe. I breathe in the smell of it, and my voice comes as a whisper.

"It's snowing."

14.

The last time I saw snow was maybe when I was eleven or twelve. I remember getting up early and listening to the local radio station while I ate Lucky Charms and waited for them to call off school. It was only a few inches, but it was enough to make a big bowl of what my mom called "snow cream" and for me and Eleanor to sled on a trash can lid straight into our neighbor's ditch, over and over, until our feet were pins-and-needles numb. We lived in our pajamas and watched movies for days.

That nostalgic, magic feeling is the first that tingles through me as I stand on the porch, watching big flakes falling fast. In the dark, away from the glow of the streetlight, it almost looks dainty, the way the white flecks dance before settling onto the ground. Everything is already powdered-sugar dusted. It has settled in the tall pines and frosted the wide magnolia leaves, and there's no sign of this stopping.

The second feeling that runs through me is a more immediate panic, one that all Southerners know and laugh about every winter: I don't have any milk or bread. Aside from the fact that both of those items were probably sold out by noon today and that I'm not exactly sure how either would sustain me through a freeze, I also can't remember the last time I went to the grocery store. My fridge is a barren wasteland of condiments. I was planning to take care of this tomorrow. For some reason, when I realize this, I begin to laugh.

Miles looks at me like I'm crazy, and I might be. I ease out onto the steps and let the snow settle onto my sweater and into my hair. Everything about the moment already feels different. It's not just the change in color and composition, but the soft, peaceful wonder of it.

I need to get my camera. I need to put on my coat. I need to turn around and tell him the truth.

When I glance back towards the house, I find him looking at the sky, and his hands, and really anything but me.

"I'm sorry," I say. "You're right. I just don't want you to be right. About... why I'm alone. For Christmas."

The words stumble out of me with a foggy sigh. A few more hazy clouds leave my mouth before he replies.

"I'm sorry, too." I know he doesn't just mean about being right. "And you're not alone."

My smile comes on as soft and slow as the falling snow. "Truce?"

He narrows his eyes at me. "What's the catch?"

I shrug over-dramatically, like a sparkly-sweet character in a cartoon world.

"Go for a walk with me?"

He laughs like I'm either the cutest thing he's ever seen or the most impossible. Both are maybe true. Snow prickles my cheeks. It's close to midnight, and I half-expect him to head into the warmth of his house and say no.

Major Tom has ventured out onto the porch to inspect. He sits on the top step and swishes his tail, watching the falling flakes with the quiet amusement of one who sees things like this all the time. I almost expect him to yawn as Miles scoops him up and heads for the open door.

"Let me get my coat."

***

In fifteen minutes, the grass is a thin blanket of white. In thirty, our feet are sinking into the sidewalk with an audible crunch. It feels like the only sound for miles. It also feels like we've walked for miles. This is entirely my fault. I always promise him a little further, and then my gaze wanders down the glittery path of another street. My nose has long since gone numb, and my mitten-clad fingers are clumsy as I snap another picture. The chunky, retro string lights lining yet another white roof cast a multi-colored glow against the misty gray sky.

"Just a few more," I promise.

"You know that scene at the end of *The Shining* where Jack Nicholson is just a human icicle?"

"We can head back," I say guiltily.

"I'm kidding. It's nice. I didn't really need these toes, anyway."

I notice, when he smiles, that crystalline flakes are clinging to his eyelashes. They dust his hair and speckle the upturned collar of his coat. If this whole night is just a dream, right now he looks the part. I fall into step and hook my arm in his -- for warmth, I think, and safety, and certainly not because of the way my heart flips when he looks at me like that.

We meander towards the next cross street, and I'm thinking we probably should head back, when three shadows dart across our path.

"Oh!" I gasp. "Did you see that?"

"What?"

I'm already dragging him by the arm until we're sprinting through the snow. The trio ahead of us picks up speed.

"Raccoons!" I say.

"Raccoons?"

"Three of them!"

I shimmy through some holly bushes at the corner and jet out into the next street. Behind me, I hear him fighting through the narrow intersection of prickly leaves. I slow to a creep, bringing a finger to my mouth to shush him.

"Are you a wildlife photographer now?" he half-whispers.

"No. But they're cute!"

"They're a menace. There's supposedly one for every three people in the city. But I guess if they're cute, it's fine?"

"People could say the same about musicians."

I hear him laugh from somewhere close behind me.

"You think I'm cute?"

I would roll my eyes, but I'm too focused on those three waddling shadows: two big and one smaller, creeping along the sidewalk up ahead.

"I think you're overpopulated."

I drop to a crouch and snap a few quick shots before sprinting away again. To be relatively rotund, they're quick. Their hunched backs and full tails remind me of Major Tom, except slightly bigger, and darker, and more feral. I'm halfway down the next street when I catch them disappearing into the storm drain. Even though I know this is basically the city subway system for trash pandas, I almost can't believe it. They squeeze through in quick succession. By the time I catch up to them, with the cold burning in my lungs, all that's left is a trail of little clawed footprints. I take a picture of it anyway.

"See any scary clowns down there?" Miles asks as I double back in defeat.

"No, but I think they're in cahoots."

"Yeah. He's probably using them as bait."

"Bait for what?" I laugh.

"To lure unsuspecting girls into the sewers."

"You think I'm unsuspecting."

"Of course not. I think you're entirely too suspicious of everything."

"Thanks," I deadpan.

"Oh, c'mon. It's a compliment. It happens to be one of those things I like most about you."

"My ability to avoid being snatched by a serial killer?"

"Your complete inability to agree with anything I say."

I don't know how to take this, but I know that the way he says it makes me want to smile. I adjust the settings on my camera instead, careful not to trip on the crossties as we make the block at the railroad crossing. We haven't heard the familiar bellow of a train for hours, and the corridor is long and lined with quiet pines. That untouched white path stretches all the way to the next intersection, where the traffic lights glow like those dozens of rooftops already frozen forever in my photo reel.

"I can't believe it's snowing," I say for the hundredth time.

"Holly Danford wasn't convincing enough for you?"

"I don't think I trust anyone with teeth that white."

"I never knew you were such a skeptic."

I consider that I hadn't really realized I was such a skeptic, either. Growing up, I'd believed I could have the world and conquer it, too. I guess at some point over the past year, reality crept up on me. That no matter how careful you are or how much work you put in, plans still fail, and hearts still break, and life still isn't anything like the ones you see on TV, where those couples in my age group earned their million-dollar starter-home budgets by following their dreams of selling wine cork reindeer. What a fucking year.

"I'm almost thirty," I sigh. "I guess it's about time, right?"

"Time for what?"

"To stop believing in impossible things. Like Santa Claus. And love. And happily-ever-afters."

"And snow?" he says.

That smirk sneaks up the back of my neck, as if he's running his fingers along my spine. He was right, that night on the roof. Why is he always right? The space between us feels magnetic, and I add a little more, wondering how far away I have to be before my body doesn't respond to his proximity.

"Sometimes snow is inevitable," I say. "It's just science. Cold fronts and weather patterns."

"And love isn't?"

I almost choke on my laugh.

"You're gonna talk to me about love?"

"I'm a little offended at how hilarious you find this to be."

"Okay, I'm talking about love, not 'love'." My air quotes are unsuccessful given the fact that I'm wearing mittens; I end up looking like a dramatic ninja turtle. "That random late-night stuff doesn't count."

"Random late-night stuff," he says. "Like this?"

I shoot him a look. "You know what I mean."

He looks entirely too amused as we veer down the salted sidewalks of the neighborhood business district. The street between us and Matilda's glitters.

"I'm just trying to figure out what kind of love you've been making that you're using air quotes," he argues.

"Okay, Usher," I say. "I don't think anybody calls it 'making love' anymore."

"What would you prefer I call it? Gettin' jiggy with it?"

My frozen face actually hurts from how hard I'm laughing.

"Wow," I cough. "Ya know, I think I would prefer you just admit you're not looking to settle down. That you're just... using these girls."

"Are those my only options?"

I roll my eyes at him. I wonder if all guys play this game: the "maybe I'll marry you or maybe I won't, but you won't know for sure until you've wasted a few years of your life on me".

"What else is there?" I question.

I venture into the middle of the snowy street, lifting my camera and taking a shot straight down the center. He gazes into the night with his hands buried in his pockets. I take a few steps back, and the click of my camera seems to echo as I snap one of him. He glances over with the hint of a smile. His eyes dip over my mouth and wrap around the ends of my hair. He comes up and takes the camera, aiming it at my mute distrust with a click.

"Has it ever occurred to you," he says, passing it back, "that maybe they were using me?"

There's a resignation in his tone. My gaze is searching, and he holds it the way he held my hand as I dragged him off the Dennison's living room dance floor. His steps carry him toward the intersection, where a red light glows. I watch him for a moment before pulling up the last image.

I study that girl like I don't know her, even though she's got my mother's heart-shaped face and my father's straight nose. Her cheeks are pink, her knit hat is flecked with snow, and I can almost see that old spark, despite the jaded tinge of her level stare and the way her arms are folded across her chest. She's got no rings, no attachments, and no reason not to be alone in this frame. She's so very different from the girl she was last year. More fractured in some ways, stronger in others. She's a little wary and way too guarded. But she's smiling. And I wonder, when I see it, why she's still fighting it.

15.

In the weeks that followed that kiss on the moonlit rooftop, I couldn't tell if I was avoiding him or he was avoiding me. I always seemed to catch glimpses of him climbing into his car or disappearing through his door. We'd spent years like this, so I'm not sure why this felt any different, but it was. Different. I found myself lying in bed, breathing quiet, the way you do when you're listening for murderers or monsters, and hoping to catch snippets of his sounds next door. There weren't many. For the first time in four years, he was a model neighbor. Quiet. Unobtrusive. Using his own recycling bin.

I told myself, when I started plugging in headphones and listening to those playlists, that it was just for the sake of normalcy. His piano chords had always been the background of my life here, and too many other things had changed, but this piece was as easy to find as hitting play. These verses felt like a long-kept secret, one I'd dragged out a thousand times in my car or with those headphones on, while I was headed across town for a shoot or holed up in my office editing projects, so no one would overhear me listening to them.

At first it was an idle curiosity. Maybe I wanted to prove to myself that he was all those uninspired things I imagined him to be. The thing is, he was good. He had this way of writing songs that made you wish you'd written them. Songs that made you want to go for a late-night drive like you're sneaking out and seventeen, that felt like sliding into a favorite pair of worn-out jeans, that begged you to sit with a glass of wine on your porch when a storm's rolling in. They found their way into my playlists like a guilty pleasure, and any time they came on when Joss or Nate was nearby, I skipped the track, because I didn't want to explain.

I would never tell him this. I couldn't take the self-satisfied smile that would creep across his face. Heat rose in my cheeks even thinking about it. How many girls had done exactly this? Listened to these lines and felt they knew him? Felt like *he* knew them? Still, I always came back to it.

We're all just bones and strings, beating hearts and unsaid things.

It was my favorite line. I found myself singing it in the shower and jotting it into the margins of my notebook. I told myself it was because he'd tucked it into a melody that you couldn't help but lean into, like a well-laid musical trap, just another one of his tricks. Really, though, I knew why it got me. In those secret kisses he had crept into my bones, pulled my strings so tightly I could still feel that gentle tug, like he'd wrapped one around his fingers when they threaded through my hair and hadn't let go, until it became this constant line of tension between us.

Lately, my world had been filled up with unsaid things. All those hard conversations that Nate and I had skirted past, that seemed to echo off the walls of this half-empty apartment. The grief that I would carry in my body longer than I even carried that child, the details of which I hadn't shared with my mom, or my sister, or my friends. Whatever had happened between me and Miles, and whatever it meant, or didn't mean.

Bones, and strings, and unsaid things.

I was listening to it a few days after Thanksgiving when I heard the knock on my door. I tugged a headphone out of my ear with my heart racing, wondering if somehow he had heard me playing it, even though that was ridiculous. These walls were thin, but they were still walls. I swiveled out of my office chair and opened the door anyway, half-expecting to find him standing there. Instead, it was a woman, wearing a long, sable coat that reminded me of Margot Tenenbaum.

"Hey, baby," she smiled. "Is Miles around?"

I blinked at her for a moment. She was middle-aged, with a pretty face that was too heavily made up. I'd seen all kinds of girls come looking for him, but never one like this. Her hair was sandy with grunge-era bangs, but her eyes were bright blue, lined with thick spidery lashes. They danced over me, past me, into my apartment. I held more tightly to the edge of the door, wedging my foot behind it.

"Oh. Actually he doesn't –"

"I know he doesn't want to see me," she interrupted. "But I'm only in town for today, and if you'd just be a sweetheart and –"

She was already putting a manicured hand on my arm, crowding up close to me so I could smell her perfume, an old Victoria's Secret fragrance I wasn't even sure they made anymore, when Miles opened his door.

"Samantha." His features were hard as he stepped outside, with the tense line of his jaw matching the sharp edge of his tone. "What are you doing here?"

"Hey, baby," she cooed, slipping away from me easily. "Look at you! I was in the neighborhood, ya know? Just stopping by to see you. See your place."

He glanced past her now to where I was standing. He hadn't

looked me in the eyes in a month, but when he did I knew this wasn't something he wanted me to see. I glanced away, looking instead at the new SUV parked out front.

"That's not my place."

"Well, I couldn't remember which one –"

"Just... go inside."

He said it like someone who was on the verge of a migraine. He was holding the door open now, watching her saunter through it. She paused to give me a sweet smile and a little waggle of those red shellac nails.

"Sorry, sweetie," she offered. To him she added, "She's cute. Do you know her?"

"She's my neighbor. Of course I know her."

We were still standing there after she'd disappeared inside. I could hear her already, complimenting his artwork and running her fingers across the keys of his piano. Something flickered across his face at that sound: almost a wince, almost a grimace. His cheeks were pink with embarrassment, or anger, or some emotion I couldn't place.

"Sorry," he said.

"Sure," I nodded.

He was almost back inside when he stepped back out, still wearing that pained expression.

"This... never happened, okay?"

He didn't wait for my response before disappearing for good. I felt the subtle slam of the door all the way from where I stood. Heat bloomed in my face. Was that even necessary? I rolled my eyes before I eased my own door shut. Back in my office chair, I could hear the tones of their conversation.

"What are you really doing here, Sam?"

"It's Thanksgiving. Thanksgiving is for family."

"Since when are we a family?"

My curiosity mingled with a stinging sense of shame. I

couldn't listen to this, as much as I wanted to know: who she was, why he didn't want her here, everything about him. That was the dangerous part about Miles, how much I wanted to know him, despite the way he seemed entirely reckless with relationships. I couldn't rebound with him. Couldn't fall for all his lines. I was better than this, some girl who just fell into the arms of the next guy who came along, instead of being what I should have been with Nate: more careful. This is what had always gotten me through in life. This is what would keep me safe: that cautious nature that kept me from following scary clowns into snowy gutter drains. Rules, and lists, and plans.

"Why can't you ever let anything go?" she asked.

"Where were you when he was sick, Samantha? Where were you when he died?"

"I came for the funeral!"

"I'm not talking about the funeral. Dying is more than just a fucking funeral."

I don't know why chills ran up my arms, as if this conversation had anything to do with me. I'd never heard him sound like this before: serious, angry, hurt. For a flicker of a moment he wasn't just a flirty frontman or my asshole neighbor, and the thought occurred to me that if you opened him up, like the back of a piano, there'd be a hammering heart and all his strings. Same as me.

Major Tom jumped into my lap a few moments later. My mute surprise melted into a softening sigh. He kneaded his oversized paws a few times before settling in, and I smoothed a hand over his back, feeling his old man bones and the rattle of his purr. I hooked those headphones back into my ears and pressed play.

16.

HAS IT EVER OCCURRED TO ME THAT THEY WERE USING HIM?

No. Not really.

I watch footprints fill up the space between me and Miles and wonder what I really know about him. I know a few girls he's dated. I know some of the songs he sings. I know I've wondered how it would feel to be on the other side of that wall, sighing out his name.

I think about all those girls propping their boobs against his piano, and the way he sips his drinks politely. I think about those breakup stories he shared when he was picking ceramic out of my foot, and how heartbreakers don't usually plan romantic horseback rides, do they? I think about the way he looked at me when I pulled away from him at that Halloween party.

"This never happened."

I remember the flash of surprise on his face when I first

brought Nate to my place. I remember the way I had scoffed at the idea he'd be shocked that someone finally wasn't falling all over herself to become one of his groupies. I remember how he breathed into my hair on that rooftop, like I was such a relief.

When I catch up with him, he's staring up at the patch of sky between the square of red lights and green.

"It looks like Christmas," I offer.

He extends a hand. "Dance with me?"

"Is this another one of your traditions?" I smile.

"No, but they do it in *The Notebook*."

It gets easier every time, the way my gloved hand fits into his, and how his arm circles around my waist. It's warmer up against him. I press my face into his shoulder and sway to his imaginary beat, appreciating that it's much slower and simpler than the merengue and that, this time, the snowflakes are real. They waft around us like confetti, and it feels like we're standing in the middle of a snowglobe.

"You know that story is sad, right?" I say. "They die at the end."

"Spoiler alert: we all die at the end."

"Romantic," I deadpan. "What's next? You're gonna build me a house with your bare hands?"

"You would not wanna live in anything I built. But I could maybe write you a song."

"Isn't that a bit cliche?" I ask, scrunching up my nose.

"Probably. And I've got plenty more where that came from," he laughs.

The snowy night holds us in a suspended reality, one in which I don't care that I'm way too close to this guy I've spent almost four years keeping my distance from. Infatuation isn't supposed to last this long, is it? I guess I always expected that at some point it would go away, that one day I wouldn't notice that imperceptible little thrill that runs through me whenever he looks at me. There were times my awareness of it faded, sure, but it never took much to rekindle it, as if the space between us was always speckled with embers. Here – caught up in a dance that is so clearly an excuse to be against each other – I wonder why I've ever needed an excuse. Really, though, I know the answer to that.

"If I ask you something," I say, "will you tell me the truth?"

He swirls us around.

"Sure."

"Did you sleep with Jenna?"

His exhale of a laugh plays across my neck.

"What? God no," he replies. "What makes you think that?"

"That night. Three years ago. After your party."

He almost loses the beat for a second, but he recovers.

"No," he confirms. "She was too drunk to drive and slept on the couch. She's just a friend. Why?"

"Just wondering."

"You've been 'just wondering' that for three years?" he laughs. "Okay, my turn. Were you already dating Nate then?"

"I hadn't even met Nate then," I say. "Why?"

Our smiles are lingering so close I think the frozen tip of my nose might brush against his lips. Instead of a reply, he spins me out wide, until our arms are an outstretched tether. We lean against it like a trust fall, and I stare down the link at him. He reels me back in, and my heart drops, and I think for a moment he might kiss me. Instead, he knits us together at the hands, with our arms crossed at the wrists.

"Are you ready?" he asks.

"For what?"

He leans back and counterbalances my weight against his. "Don't let go."

I exhale a breathy laugh as we begin to spin. The world swirls to a white-flecked haze, and the only thing that's still in focus is the way he's laughing.

"Miles!" I giggle. "Slow down!"

"If you slow down we'll fall."

"We're already going to fall!"

I feel my gloved hands slipping, feel the cold stinging my face as we laugh, moving faster. The packing peanut sky is a blur above us, and suddenly the tether breaks. The world tilts as I tumble to the ground and sprawl out in the snow. Those slow-falling pieces float down to meet my dizzy grin. The clouds are reflective and bright as he stumbles down beside me.

"You're trying to kill me," I say.

"Me? You're the one lying in the middle of the street."

"I'm not lying in the middle of the street," I scoff.

"Then what are you doing?"

"I'm making a snow angel."

He snorts as I swish my arms and legs through the cold, even though I know I'll regret it later when I'm wet and freezing.

"And you called me cliché." Even as he says it, he settles in beside me. In another moment he's making its match. "You know what they never tell you about this? It's fucking cold."

"It's fun!"

"Fun and cold."

"You know you never answered my question," I offer.

He rolls up onto his elbow, gazing down at me. "Which one?"

"At least half of them."

Without the usual traffic, I can hear the wind in the trees. He pulls his gaze down the blanketed street. I can tell he's considering. He stares down one direction and then the other, like the answers might be waiting there. I realize not for the first time that I appreciate all his details: the kissable center of his cupid's bow, the almost dimple in his left cheek, the way his hair – now dark with dampness from the melting snow – falls across his forehead, and the way he tosses it away before he responds.

"You were right about me," he says. "I don't want to settle down."

"What's so bad about settling down?"

"What isn't? It's just that thing people do where they start listening to all their parents and friends and get scared about ending up alone forever, so they convince themselves it never gets better than whatever is in front of them. Then they tune out for the next twenty years and call it a life. I find that to be completely fucking insane. I'm not afraid of being alone. I'd rather be alone forever than spend forever with someone who makes me feel alone."

This hits me harder than it should. I watch him for a moment, considering.

"I think that's called settling," I correct.

That smirk flickers across his face. "All right. I guess, then, I don't want to settle. Is there really a difference?"

"Of course there's a difference. Settling down is more like commitment. Marriage. Family. A house in the suburbs."

"The suburbs, really? And you're telling me *that's* not settling?"

I laugh at the disgusted look on his face. "Okay, correction: a house in some swanky neighborhood where asshole musicians live. Suburbs not required."

"I don't know that I want that either," he says.

"What do you want then?"

His gaze is back on me now: those snowflake lashes and that intent blue, tugging at the depths of my soul. "Is it cliché if I say you?"

You.

It quickens through my veins. Beneath that playful expression, I can see the bare truth of it. *You.* Not just tonight. Not just in his bed. But possibly... now, and before, and always. I realize we're here, at this literal and metaphorical crossroads. I wonder how long we're going to keep dancing around this. Literally. Figuratively. He's still watching me as I bite into my bottom lip.

"Yes," I admit.

He nods. In a breath he is already beginning to shift away, like he's unsurprised to find this is the same as every other night. In another I'm snagging the front of his coat, tugging that gaze back towards me, because this time I can't let it go. This night. This moment. Him.

God, what am I doing?

It's not just his eyes on me now. It's his hands, and his breath, and that frosty exhale of surprise as I lean in. My heart is wild in my throat, and my voice comes as a sultry whisper.

"Say it anyway."

His mouth ghosts across mine. I feel him breathe in, feel the brush of his parted lips, testing, teasing.

"I want you," he says.

His words spread through me until I ache. The tip of his frozen nose nuzzles mine. He threads his hands into my hair and angles my mouth against his. His lips are cold but our kisses are warm. His tongue teases mine like he can't taste enough of me. We pull each other closer still.

"What are we doing?" I murmur.

"What do you wanna do?"

For most of my life, wants have been such a strategic thing. I wanted to move to the city. I wanted to be a photographer. I wanted a picture-perfect life and someone to spend it with. It had always been a grocery list of things I was checking off. Lying here in the snow with Miles, I realize how insane that seems, because the only thing I really want in this moment is him. It's not at all strategic. It's cold fronts and weather patterns. If I only get one night, I want this one, bathed in white. This one that defies all logic and time and space.

"You," I breathe.

The sound that escapes him is somewhere between a laugh, a groan, and a feeling that floods hot and electric through me. His words rasp against my kisses. He nips at my bottom lip.

"Are you fucking with me, Cecilia?"

When he says it like that, the syllables of my name seem to seep into my skin.

"No. Yes. I don't know how to answer that."

He's framing my face in his hands again. His mouth grazes mine, and these almost-maybe kisses are driving me crazy. I sigh against his parted lips. I want to drink in his heat and the snowy, sexy smell of him.

"Come home with me," he breathes.

Any justification I've ever had for saying no feels faraway, so I don't even try. I kiss him again.

His tongue teases mine. "Does that mean yes?"

"Yes," I smile.

I'm biting at his lip, and he's pulling me to my feet, and I'm dusting off the snow. I tuck myself against his arm, letting the scene settle around us. The traffic lights cycle from red, to yellow, to green. We leave nothing but footprints and those two messy angels in the middle of that snowglobe street.

17.

"SO WHEN I PROMISED I wasn't going to con you out of your clothes," he begins, sliding me out of my coat.

His apartment feels like the tropics compared to the hour we've spent outside. The little Christmas tree is still glowing warmly, and the low lamps burn through the room, casting us in seductive shadows.

"Don't worry," I smile. "I'm perfectly capable of taking them off myself."

I slide my scarf away from my neck and shrug out of my sweater in one smooth movement, dropping them on the floor as I drift across the room. I swipe my unfinished glass of wine off the piano and watch the way his eyes follow with a desperate sort of intensity as I raise it to my lips. I take a slow sip if only to torture him with a dramatic pause.

"You're definitely fucking with me," he smirks, leaning against the edge of the piano.

"Am I?" I tease.

I step out of my damp boots and peel off my leggings –

slowly, deliberately, like I'm doing a snow day strip tease – and I am mostly teasing, but his intent gaze rakes along my body, and a quiet thrill runs through me. It makes me believe I can be this girl – that I am this girl. The one who feels bold and brave and, when he looks at me like that, really fucking sexy.

"What about your rules?" he asks.

The question is a purr in his throat, and it draws me closer. He's wearing a look like he wants to keep undressing me. To take off this camisole and button-front skirt. To slip off everything underneath them. And I want him to. I want to feel his hands on me, his lips, his skin. But I leave that sliver of space between us.

"I thought you didn't have to touch me to make you want you," I say.

His gaze tugs through me again.

"I don't," he smirks. "But touching you is so much more fun."

I exhale a breathy laugh. He is already inching his fingers beneath the edge of my shirt. He smooths a hand across my lower back, tugging me against him. It feels so good to be against him that for a second I can't do anything but breathe him in. I smooth my hands up his chest, over his shoulders, along his jaw, just to make sure he's real. Another shaky sigh escapes me.

Yeah, he's definitely real.

Real enough that he leans in slowly, licking his tongue along my bottom lip, then the top. He plays at the parted crease between them, grazing his mouth against mine, just close enough that I can't quite catch him. Those shaky sighs become soft little moans. I can't help it. It completely fucking kills me when he does this. He knows it, too. By the time I snag his lip between my teeth, I'm nothing but desperate liquid heat. He groans into the hard, hungry way I kiss him.

"Fuck," I murmur. "You're really good at this."

"You sound surprised."

The way I almost laugh is lost to his lips. He's inching off my top, and I'm fumbling with his belt, and I love the way he's kissing me, like it'll never be enough. His mouth hovers above the sensitive spot where my neck meets my shoulder, and I feel my head tip involuntarily, offering it up to him. He doesn't take it. I almost moan when he doesn't. His exhale warms across my skin. He's so close I can feel the heat radiating off of him as he nuzzles my pulse point. I arch against him with a tiny groan.

"Where did we land on touching, again?"

"Good," I say. "Really good."

He drags his fingers along the back of my neck, over my shoulder, between the swell of my breasts. My nipples harden in response. He moves so slowly, like he wants to map all of my most sensitive spots and memorize the exact way I respond when he touches me. Throbbing heat pools between my legs in a way that's impossible to ignore.

"Just good?" he teases.

His smile ghosts across my skin, and I wonder if I've ever gotten off from making out, because I'm already too close. He kisses me like he can taste it. His fingers play along the edge of my bra. He slides the straps over my shoulders, one after another, like I'm a gift he's taking pleasure in unwrapping. Every part of me responds to his touch. He bites my neck, my shoulder, slowly tugs away the flimsy fabric, until my breasts are bare between us. He cups his hands up them, tracing his thumbs across the hard peaks of my nipples. Those blue eyes dip into mine, and I can see him savoring the way I respond as he strokes the taut, sensitive, rose-colored flesh.

I moan as another wave of pleasure surges through me, realizing only belatedly that I was supposed to respond. I weave my fingers into his hair with a smooth, velvety sigh.

"Really fucking good," I manage.

He draws one of my nipples into his mouth, sucking just until my legs go weak. He can't stay still, and he's teasing my lips against his again, and his hands are all over me. In my hair, caressing my breasts, burning across the sensitive curve of my low back.

"You're not even fair," he breathes.

Even as he says it, I wonder if he can see how much I need him. Because I really, *really* need him. The words come as an incomprehensible sound that gets caught against his mouth. I'm not sure if I think it, or breathe it, or moan it, but I'm reaching for him. I catch that shudder of breath when I stroke down the plane of his stomach, hear that throaty growl when I slide inside his boxers and grip the full, solid length of him.

Holy fuck, yes.

The confirmation aches through me: he's got a great cock. As if it's even possible, he gets harder against my touch. I work my hand up and down for a few breaths, reveling in the masculine feel of him. He grips into the suede softness of my skirt, squeezing the supple curve of my ass.

"God, Cecilia," he groans.

He's already scooping me up the way I wouldn't let him that night in my kitchen, with my legs wrapped around his middle and him hard against me. He is so impossibly sexy, and we're kissing against the wall, and stumbling into a lamp, and crashing into an end table. He drops me across that red velvety chair, with my skirt up around my hips and his mouth trailing kisses along my inner thigh. He drags his gaze over me again, and I've never felt so exposed, and I've never wanted anything more than the way his fingers slide along my hip, just beneath the edge of my underwear.

"Not black," he smirks.

"You've thought about this?" I ask.

"You haven't?"

And somehow I'm half-naked, and laughing, and aching, and sighing.

"God you're such a jerk," I say, but I'm pulling him up to meet me, or is he pulling me to meet him?

He tugs me to the edge of that chair as those little burgundy, lace-lined hipsters slip down my thighs and get lost somewhere on the floor. He smooths down my legs until they're inviting him in, and he hooks the backs of my knees over the arms of that chair, one after another.

My god.

He moves up my body like I am entirely edible. How does anyone have this much self control? Mine is melting away with every press of his mouth against my hips, my stomach, my breasts. He kisses up the swell of them, teases my nipples with lazy flicks of his tongue.

"Am I," he whispers, gently tugging one between his teeth. "Such a jerk?"

Fucking fuck.

He moves to the other, licking and biting in a slow, teasing rhythm, like he never wants me to stop making this sound. That snowball fight glitter from his face shimmers across my skin with every little movement.

How is this even real? This desperate ache. This need that seems to be winding itself through my very soul.

"Fuck, I want you," I breathe.

He kisses me deeply as his hand slides slowly between my legs.

"Say it again," he murmurs.

His thumb circles the swollen, sensitive mound of my clit teasingly, coaxing me until I lose my breath. Words feel like a faraway concept, but I grasp for them, on the verge of panting.

"I want you so fucking bad."

I'm arching into his touch, and every nerve in my body has turned to fire, and I love being spread open for him.

"Want me to what?"

I grind against him, and I know he knows what. The heat rises in my face anyway. I'm asking with my eyes and my body and the press of my fingernails, gripping into his shoulders.

"Oh my god please."

He strokes me in tantalizing little circles as if in response. Pleasure surges through me again, pushing me towards the edge. He's moving just right, playing me like one of his songs, and I can't even form words. If I was on the other side of this wall I doubt I'd even hear the sounds that escape me, because they're so quiet, and so desperate, and why won't he just –

"You know I wanted you from the first time I saw you," he says. "Sexy. Screaming. No bra."

His free hand traces the curve of my breasts, rolling one of those hard peaks between his thumb and forefinger.

"I wanted to taste your perfect tits. And watch you take off those sexy little shorts."

Oh my god.

"Bend you over. Hear you beg."

The sound that escapes me is nothing more than a gasp, a whimper, a plea. He teases my slit, up and down.

"Feel you come."

He slides a finger inside me, then another, stroking deeper, dragging his teeth across that little indentation above my hip. Jolts of pleasure course through me.

"Is this how you make yourself come when you think about fucking me?"

A strangled sound escapes me.

Yes. God yes.

Those secret thoughts burn through me, all the times I've imagined him in my bed, thrusting into me as he worked my clit, fucking me in the shower. This is so much better. I don't even have the breath to tell him how much I need him to fuck me – hard, and fast, and right goddamn now – when he brings his tongue between my legs.

"Oh *fuck*," I sigh. "I need you to... Miles... *Fuck*..."

He's enjoying this too much to stop. He nuzzles against the slick heat of me, licking, teasing, tasting. He's still toying with my nipples, still stroking the sensitive spot inside me, mimicking the hard press of his cock. I feel him groan, feel him lashing his tongue against my clit in that taunting rhythm that matches the way my heart is pounding, pounding, pounding. My breaths come quick and desperate.

There. I'm right there.

I'm writhing against him, shameless and moaning, when tidal waves of hot, perfect pleasure crash through me. He licks at me in satisfaction, until the feeling is just a tremor, gently quaking through my core. I'm still breathing out desperate little sounds as he tugs me up to meet him.

"You said you needed something?" he teases.

I melt into him as I laugh.

"You," I say. I sound drunk, as if the feel of him has completely flooded my brain. He smooths his hand along my thigh and wraps it around his torso, kissing me once, twice. "Fuck, I need you."

He tugs me towards him, but I'm entirely liquid. In another instant we're tumbling into the floor, and he sinks against the rug, taking me with him. It feels so good to be on top of him. My body is still throbbing, still aching, and I arch my hips against his. He's nipping at my neck and tracing down my wrists, catching my fingers before I can wrap them around the hard length of him. Instead he teases them into his mouth, one after another.

"Not fair," I groan.

He meets my quiet protest with a kiss.

"We've got time," he whispers. "I'll catch up."

18.

Time we indeed have plenty of. Some other critical items? Not so much.

"You're sure?" I sigh, as we rifle through the contents of his bathroom cabinet. He snakes his arms around me from behind. "You checked everywhere? Your wallet? Your car? Your bedside table?"

"Everywhere," he confirms.

My groan tugs a laugh out of him.

"I'm sorry to disappoint you, but I don't really do this as often as you imagined. And I didn't exactly plan this."

"What's that whole thing about, ya know, being prepared?"

"I think that's the boy scouts," he says, running his hands down my front.

"A fine motto," I sigh.

He is already kissing my neck and nipping at my ear. Everything about this makes me want him inside me, and every time he gets me off makes me want him much more still.

"You don't have anything at your place?"

"Anything that's not dangerously past its expiration date?"

I know there is an almost zero point zero percent chance that I have anything. Despite Joss's complete distaste for the topic, I decided a few months back that celibacy was the only way to go. I now understood exactly why she'd given me that look like I'd lost my entire fucking mind.

It was really the anxiety that had done it. Or rather, the herbal supplement I'd started taking for the anxiety. She had found it sitting innocently in my kitchen cabinet, a few weeks after Nate left. I'd started taking it right after Christmas, when the whole world began to feel like it was made up of hard edges and my soul started to feel like a sensitive bruise on your hip that keeps snagging the corner of the kitchen table in just the wrong way. My pictures felt uninspired. My conversations felt insincere. My brain felt disconnected, and I couldn't figure out why. I chalked it up to a quarter-life crisis.

I considered later that maybe my body knew what my mind had yet to accept: that Nate and I weren't in love anymore. We were just a really convincing snapshot of a couple who smiled when they showed up at backyard parties and dinners and work functions with color-coordinating clothes and convincing conversations.

"When I open my restaurant," Nate would say.

"When we get married," I would offer.

Everything good was a when, stretched out somewhere in the hazy dreamland ahead of us, I guess to distract from the fact that the now was just... pretend.

It was only our second Christmas together, but he'd been hinting heavily at a ring. So heavily, in fact, that he'd called Joss to get my size.

"I think the bastard's really gonna do it," she'd laughed on the phone with me, right after he swore her to secrecy. "He's planning Christmas morning, at your parents' house. The only problem is he's still talking diamonds."

"Okay, as my best friend, I'm gonna need you to talk him out of that," I said. "But holy shit, is this really happening?"

"That's what he says."

When I opened that jewelry-sized box on Christmas morning, with butterflies in my stomach and my hands shaking, it contained a heart-shaped necklace that didn't look like anything I would remotely ever wear. I was an earrings girl. Sometimes a cute bracelet girl. Never a heart-shaped necklace girl.

"Do you love it?" he asked.

I had tears in my eyes when I smiled, and he read it exactly the way he wanted to.

It's not that he didn't propose; it's that he'd clearly wanted to, and then he hadn't. And I couldn't figure out what had changed in those few months, how he'd gone from someone who wanted to marry me to someone I wasn't sure knew me.

After he was gone, and Joss sat the bottle on my counter with a heavy look, I stilled, wondering if she was about to tell me that it had been linked to blood clots, or cancer, or irreparable brain damage.

"About this," she began.

"Yes," I said warily.

"This is the why."

"Why what?"

"Why the pill stopped working."

I stared at it for a second before sinking onto the barstool. I picked up the bottle. I knew before I turned it over that I'd already read the entire label, because I always double-checked things like that. It hadn't come with a warning: may derail your entire life.

"Damn," I said. "I feel..."

Like an idiot, I thought. But I didn't say it, because Joss was already shaking her head

"You should feel relieved. Because now you know. And this?" she said, rattling the bottle for emphasis. "This told you the truth sooner than he would have."

"Why does the truth always have to be like that?"

"Be like what?"

"Hard?" I grimace. "You know, how they always say 'the hard truth'. Why can't the truth ever just be… easy?"

She snorted a laugh, but her hand found mine with a gentle squeeze.

"I dunno. I guess so you remember."

"Lesson learned," I sighed. "Stop sleeping with lying bastards. Actually, stop sleeping with everyone."

"Okay," she'd warned, "let's not get dramatic."

But I committed. I quit the pills, all of them, and started going to therapy. I threw myself into work and considered getting a dog. I was completely fine, living my very sexless existence, until my asshole neighbor made me come on his couch. And in his bed. And almost again in his kitchen, after we gave up searching for that box of condoms he swore didn't exist.

We need a distraction. Somewhere between two o'clock and three, I decide that French toast with him in the middle of the night is the next best thing. His kitchen is fully stocked with milk and bread and eggs, and cinnamon-sugar breakfast dishes are an excellent distraction. I hope.

"It's just regular ol' American bread," he says. "Not one of those fancy ones with a French name."

"In my family, we always make it with regular ol' American bread," I grin. "It's tradition."

I'm wrapped in his robe, which I didn't hesitate pointing out is black when he draped it around me.

"What's with you and all the black, anyway?" he asks.

"Oh, you've finally decided it has nothing to do with

matching my soul?"

"It's still on the table. I don't hear any auxiliary reasons."

I crack an egg into the bowl, giving him a look.

"I do actually wear stuff that isn't black, in case you haven't noticed."

He smirks, and I smile, remembering that he has actually noticed.

"I'm a photographer, remember? Dark colors don't reflect light. And it matches everything," I say. "What's your excuse?"

"Me?"

"You and all your old man sweaters."

"Sweaters are not just for old men," he defends. "Hemingway wore sweaters."

"You did not just compare yourself to Hemingway."

"I think the comparison ends there," he admits. "I guess if we're being honest, I got them the same way I ended up with that piano. Hand-me-downs from my grandfather."

"Like, literally?"

"Some of them," he shrugs.

I whisk the egg wash in a bowl. "Tell me about him."

"I was named after him: Thomas Miles. He's the reason I moved back here. The reason I became a teacher. He was just... a genuinely good person. He always did the right thing. He would've really liked you."

"Why's that?"

"Because he also had strong feelings about *love*," he says, adding ironic air quotes. "He was always telling me that one day I was going to realize it isn't something you can find in a song."

"And you told him he was wrong?"

"Of course not. He was my grandfather. I told him I hoped he was right. And he would always wink at me – it was this thing he did – and say he knew he was. Right. But I'm a hard sell."

"What happened?" I ask softly.

"Cancer."

Even though he shrugs, I can hear the gravity in his voice. He lightens it with a half-smile.

"When I moved back, he told me he could die just fine without my help. I guess he thought I had better things to do than sit around playing cards with an old man, but honestly, I was burned out on touring, and I couldn't let him do it alone. Not the dying, but the living. I guess because there were so many times he made sure I didn't have to do it alone."

I find myself watching him for a moment. His honesty creeps up my arms and weaves between my ribs, and I can't explain how it looks so good on him. That open face and those faraway blues.

"But yeah," he adds, bringing us back to his earlier point. "I look damn good in those sweaters."

"So modest."

"Modesty is entirely overrated."

I'm flipping the first batch of toast when he comes up behind me and brings his smile to my neck, stringing kisses along my skin. His hands rove down my waist, under the belt of his robe. I'm not wearing underwear, and he takes full advantage, slipping his fingers along my sensitive, still-wet center. He seems perfectly fine going for that triple play, and as much as I love it, I groan.

"I'm just gonna go next door and check," I say.

"Stay," he whispers.

I'm already passing him the spatula and moving for the door, and he's side-stepping with me, curling his fingers up my neck.

"What about the toast? You should not trust me with this."

"I'll be right back."

"Mm-mm," he argues. "If you leave it might break the spell."

"What spell?"

He kisses me, and I smile, knowing exactly what he means. It's that instant-matchlight-chemistry that got me naked on his couch and drew me into his bed, where, wrapped up in his sheets, he reminded me of all the ways he didn't have to fuck me to get me off. Still, I want him. Under me. On top of me. And I can't handle the knowledge that the stores are all closed, possibly for *days*.

"Two minutes," I say. "Pour me a drink?"

He watches me jingle my keys and disappear into the cold of the back porch, where everything is frosty and my bare feet are already freezing as I fumble with the lock. The flakes are fewer now, but they're still drifting through the dark like a cottonwood breeze. I decide, if I can't secure any sex, that I'm going to make him sit with me out here, just to watch it snow.

I don't even flip on the light as I let myself inside, swinging into the bathroom and checking under the sink. I'm not surprised when I come up empty, but I'm cursing anyway.

"Fuck," I say. "Fucking fuck."

I consider the bedside table. I breeze into my room, and I'm already on my knees, rummaging through the side drawer, when I hear a sleepy groan.

It's instinctive, the way I scream. In a single scurry I'm up against the wall, flailing for the lightswitch, but when I flip it on, all I can see is an unidentified lump in my bed, and all I can do is scream again. I grab a picture frame off the dresser and throw it at the shifting form before I spot the sleeve of tattoos. He shoots up with his pomade hair sticking out at odd angles, screaming too.

"What the actual..." I gasp. "Oh my god, you've got to be fucking kidding me."

Nate is taking me in, partially dusted with glitter and standing here in Miles's robe, and I pull it more tightly around my chest, as if it can slow the way my heart is hammering against it.

"Did you break into my house?" I ask incredulously.

"What? No. I have a key. I texted you."

"No," I say, rejecting this.

A person should be able to delete a middle-of-the-night message without coming home to find an ex in her bed.

"C'mon, Ceil," he pleads. "I just came to talk."

"About what?!" I screech.

"You, actually," he says, rubbing the sleep off his face. "Are you doing okay? I know we haven't talked a lot lately, and I was trying to give you your space, but you just don't seem like you, and –"

"No!" I repeat, this time louder. "Do you even hear yourself? You left, Nate. You packed up, and decided you didn't love me anymore, and moved to Cali-fucking-fornia. We ended. We're through."

"This is kind of what I'm talking about," he says, motioning to me. "I never said I didn't love you. Where is that even coming from?"

I gape at him for a moment and then growl. Actually growl, as if this animalistic sound is the only thing that I can muster, because he doesn't deserve words, and I'm so sick of hearing him speak I could rip out his jugular with my teeth.

"I want you to get out. Just get the fuck out."

"Cecilia?" My name is a call of concern, coming in through the back door. I squeeze my eyes shut. Because if this could get worse, it's about to.

Suddenly, Miles is standing beside me, wide-eyed – in nothing but a coat and boxers. He's carrying a baseball bat, which he lowers as his expression shifts somewhere between stunned and unsure.

"Um..."

"It's fine," I say, and I don't know why I'm saying it, because it's so far from fine. "He's, um..."

Actually, I have no idea what he's doing. He should be leaving, but he's sitting on the edge of the bed. His sleepy gaze clears as he looks from me to Miles and back again, as if piecing together this puzzle. He starts to laugh, and it's an arrogant, disgusted kind of sound like he's spitting out cheap wine.

"I really thought you were kidding about that," he says. "Is this, like, a revenge fuck or something?"

My face warms, and I don't have time to wonder what Miles is thinking, but I'm realizing he was right about the spell-breaking, and *why* did I leave his apartment?

"No," I say.

"Should I...?" Miles begins.

"Really, Ceil?" Nate is saying. "I thought we were –"

"No!" I say again. I say it to Nate, say it to Miles, declare it to the universe itself, and suddenly I can't stand another second of this. I don't want to hear what he thinks we were, because I know what we are: over. A thousand fucking percent.

I stalk across the room, dragging Nate off my bed and not even caring if I dislocate his Mark Twain arm with the force I'm using to haul him towards the door.

"Jesus-fucking-Christ," he says, swatting me away. "You said we could still be friends."

Because I'm a nice person, I want to say. Because I am an idiot. Because I was naive enough to think that would make this whole thing easier.

Miles steps out of the way as we storm by, and the only mercy is that he doesn't try to help, because the last thing I need right now is for him to act like I need rescuing.

"Friends?" I demand. "*Friends* don't break all their goddamn promises. They don't break each other's hearts, and they sure as fuck don't break into each other's houses."

"Oh c'mon. I didn't break into your..." He tears a hand through his hair and spits out another sour laugh. "You're just pissed because I caught you fucking your neighbor."

From across the room I hear Miles laugh now, and the sound spins Nate around. Before he can start spouting off all those standard lines that preclude bro-on-bro violence, I snatch his keys off the coffee table and tear free the little gold one that he used to let himself into here. The bulk of his keyring hits him in the chest with an audible clatter.

"I can fuck whomever I damn well please. I'm not your friend. I'm not your fallback. I'm done. You can find someone else to fuck over."

I almost think, for that brief second when he's staring at me like I've just punched him in the gut, that he's going to apologize. For the first time, I realize I don't care if he does. He holds up his hands in mock surrender, before tossing a glare at Miles as he stoops to grab his keys off the floor. When he opens the door, he stands there for a long moment, staring into that cold brightness, and I realize that it's possible when he showed up here it wasn't snowing. I don't for a single breath think that's my problem.

"Merry fucking Christmas, Ceil," he says, not bothering to turn around. "Try not to get knocked up this time."

I stare at the door after it slams shut. The emotional detonation fills the apartment with that loud, ringing silence I've come to know so well. It takes a few seconds for my eyes to adjust to the dark again. In that long, quiet moment, everything is black.

19.

FOR WHAT FEELS LIKE WHOLE MINUTES, we stand in the shadowy chill of my apartment, and neither of us says anything. I realize I'm shaking. I wrap my arms around myself, and I know it's not just the cold. I feel like I'm watching this night – with its snow and seduction – slip into the realm of maybes and might-have-beens. I don't have the words for this moment.

Bones, and strings, and unsaid things.

My heart is pounding, and every string inside me is stretched so tightly it might break. Miles's tone is tentative when he asks, "I'm... a revenge fuck?"

I swallow around the receding anger and the rising desperation tightening through my throat.

"No."

It's the truth, isn't it? Maybe there's a part of me that left with him out of spite, or for the sake of warmth, or at a point of desperation, but there's another part – that secret part – that has wanted him for a long time.

"But you told him we were...?"

"I let him think it," I admit, with my face growing hot. "Earlier. At Matilda's. Before… everything."

'Everything' doesn't quite encompass it. I feel like months have passed since I was sitting at that bar. We don't close the distance between us, and my body notices it. Notices that we went from being unable to keep our hands off each other to standing on opposite sides of the room, like there's a minefield between us. My gaze wanders back to the front door, trying to figure out how we got here.

He's standing there with that unreadable expression and his hands in his pockets, and I feel like I can't breathe. The moment seems to stretch, and I know I could fill it up with words, but somehow I don't know that it would make a difference. He doesn't have to believe me. I'm just another girl. A girl who almost kissed him on his back porch and showed up the next week with a boyfriend. A girl who actually did kiss him on that downtown rooftop and told him it never happened. A girl who wanted to go home tonight with anyone but him.

"Maybe we should've asked if he had a condom."

This is not what I expect him to say.

"What?"

"I mean, 'revenge makeout' doesn't really have the same ring to it."

I blink a few times. I have no idea how to take this. I realize now that the corner of his mouth is tugging upward.

"Is everything a joke to you?" I ask.

"Not everything, but that guy? Definitely."

As annoying as it is, that crooked smile is somehow such a relief. I laugh even as my vision blurs with the threat of tears.

"You're impossible."

"What? You wanna talk about it? Because I'd love to hear you explain why your crazy ex-boyfriend was over here sleeping in your bed while you were over there, definitely not sleeping, in mine."

"Not really," I admit.

"If you'd rather fight about it, we could probably do that, too. But after seeing the way you nailed him with those keys, I dunno," he says. "Seriously, though -- where was that aim during our snowball fight?"

I am rolling my eyes at him now, fighting that smile like always. I wish I had something to throw at him right about now. He swings the baseball bat over his shoulder, running a hand through his hair. He's not exactly moving for the door, but he isn't moving towards me either. The damage that Nate intended to inflict is seemingly done. He seems to register this as it slips across my face.

"You okay?"

Even as he says it, I can hear the softening in his voice. I shrug.

"At least it didn't happen at a Chili's, right?"

"That's the spirit."

"Yeah." I swell with a breath. "So, I guess we should..."

I don't know how to finish this sentence, because I have no idea what should come next. There are a thousand ways the rest of this night can go. We can say our goodbyes and pretend we'll try again tomorrow. We can call this whole thing off and put those thin walls back between us. Or we could slip back under that spell, and revel in this after-midnight magic for just a little longer. Is that crazy?

I see him shake his head.

"Fuck 'should'," he says.

"Miles."

"Oh c'mon. It's not like there's a list. Is there? Please tell me you didn't make a list. Am I on it? 'Thou shalt not get jiggy with thy neighbor'."

I don't really know how he does it -- how he takes a moment that is anything but funny and laughs about it -- but for a moment I'm laughing too.

"Look, I shouldn't give you my opinion, but that guy never deserved a single second of the time he spent with you. And you should know that's not your fault."

That desperation is back again, tugging at my strings and seeping into my bones. I sink against the kitchen counter, digging into another one of those secret places.

"It kind of feels like my fault. I should've known. I should've —"

"Stop." Then more gently, "Stop."

I feel my eyes sting with tears now, and I stare at the door again, just to have something to do besides send them rolling down my cheeks. I feel more than see him moving towards me. When he brushes my arm, his touch is tentative. I feel the relief in his limbs as I fold myself against his chest. Every time he holds me, it's always the same: that feeling like he's wanted to do it so many times before. He threads a hand into my hair, and I press my face into the coarse wool of his coat.

"It's not your fault," he says. "Sometimes people suck. Really shitty things happen. It's not your fault. Trust me."

When I sigh, it's its own kind of response. Some of the tension loosens. Some of those strings relax. I'm worried if I thank him out loud that I'll break down crying, so instead I squeeze him a little more tightly. In some weird way I do trust him.

"But I kind of get what you meant now," he says. "About stabbing him in the throat. The fire pit cannot do him justice. It took everything in me not to break open his fucking head with this bat."

I exhale a laugh into his shoulder.

"I'm glad you didn't. Talk about a mess." I feel his laugh vibrate through me. "Plus, I can handle myself."

"I know you can," he says. The subtle certainty in his voice makes me soften into him. I've definitely questioned my ability to keep anything under control this year, but hearing the confidence in his voice is so reassuring. He smooths a hand down my hair, swaying me against him. "Can I ask you something?"

I brace myself for everything, anything. I've come this far. I sigh.

"Okay."

"Why is it so cold in here?"

Of all the things I expect, it isn't this. I ease into him with another smile.

"My furnace is on the fritz."

"Ah," he says. "Is that why you came home with me? To keep you warm?"

"Maybe."

He frames my face in his hands, and I almost think he's going to say something more, but maybe that look says it for him. I've never felt so beautiful, and so breakable, and maybe that's why he's so gentle when he brushes his nose against mine. His lips caress mine softly, slowly, the same way I slide my arms inside his coat. I still want him. Want him to keep looking at me like that and kissing me like this. I pull him closer, and his hands are sliding inside my robe again, and I'm groaning into his mouth again. I sigh a little as he pulls away.

"Do you hear that?" he says.

I hold my breath, listening. I don't know what I expect: a call, a knock, or Nate smashing in the windshield of my car. Instead, I hear a faint beeping. We share a look of confusion for a moment.

"Is that..."

It's not a wristwatch. Or an alarm clock. It almost sounds like...

We seem to realize it at the same time.

"Holy shit," he says, lunging for the door.

We are racing pulses and panic as we jet across the room. I can already smell the smoke as we clamor back into the snow.

***

What do you mean it snowed? Is that a euphemism?

Joss's message is waiting when we return, along with a few smoldering squares of something that once resembled French toast sizzling in the skillet, and Major Tom sitting on the counter, as if to casually say, "Hey guys. Nice of you to come back. Shit's on fire."

It takes us ten minutes of fanning frozen air through the back door before the smoke clears. The worst part is that this failed attempt was the last of the bread, so we've had to improvise with a backup plan.

Miles has changed into a pair of plaid pajama pants, and when he sees me standing here, watching him burn his fingers on the toaster, he smiles. I steal one of the cinnamon-sugar poptarts from the plate.

"I'll have you know I was saving these for Santa," he says.

"I'm pretty good at making lists," I offer, taking a bite. "And I have been known to check them twice."

My phone is ringing from the pocket of my robe, and I'm pulling it out as he slides onto the piano bench.

"Put me on the naughty one, will you?" he says over his shoulder.

I roll my eyes at him before I catch my mom's name lit up on the screen, which is either really good or really bad. In an instant, my thoughts are racing and my heart is thumping along after them, because – given the way my mind works – I automatically assume the latter.

"Hello?"

It's three a.m., and my voice has taken on the husky, after-midnight quality of an old school actress. My mom, however, sounds perfectly chipper, like it's three in the afternoon, and she's calling to tell me about some new tomatoes she planted in her garden.

"Oh honey, hey," she says.

"Hi. Is everything okay?"

"What? Oh. That. Yes, well, you know how these things go."

"Um, not really," I say. "What's happening? Is Ellie okay? And the baby?"

She's laughing now, the way she does when she's already "deep in her cups", as my grandmother used to say. Given that she's spent all night at the hospital, where I doubt they're serving booze, I have to assume she's been up so long that she's delirious.

"Oh, they're fine! They're fine. They think it'll be a while yet. They're wanting her to try to get some sleep, poor thing."

"Oh," I sigh, settling against the doorway. "Okay, well, what about you? And dad?"

"We're gonna go get some rest, too, I think." Then, as a dawning realization, "Why are you still up?"

"Well, you called," I offer vaguely.

She's laughing again, and now I can hear that she really is tired. I watch Miles move his fingers phantom-soft across the keys, and I wonder if he can hear the silent song in his head.

"I'm sorry," she sighs. "I love you, Cee."

"I love you, too, Mom. You'll call when something happens?"

"Of course," she agrees. "The very when."

I laugh because, even though I have no idea what she means by that, it sort of makes sense. As we say our goodbyes, the pang in my chest makes me wish I was there. Makes me wish I could talk to Ellie, to tell her everything about why I'm not there, and all the ways I know she's going to be an amazing mom. To make it make sense somehow. After I hang up, though, the songs that Miles begins to play reminds me how it's not so bad to be here, either.

I type a quick reply to Joss and hit send.

Since when is snow a euphemism? Do you mean cocaine?

She replies with a side-eye. *I meant the MAN.*

I laugh in spite of myself. I can't remember when I started referring to Miles exclusively as My Asshole Neighbor, but Joss's use of it in this particular instance is a source of amusement. As my mom has already demonstrated, though, most things are funnier at three in the morning.

The MAN just made me breakfast, I reply.

Her response comes as a five-part buzz.

Oh

My

God

What

!?!?

I can barely contain my smile. I'm already typing a reply when Miles asks, "Are you texting about me over there?"

"Not everything is about you," I defend.

This does not stop me from hitting send on 'details to come', adorned with an angel emoji, before slipping my phone into the oversized pocket of my robe. I ease onto the piano bench beside him.

"You know if I was on the other side of this wall, I'd be super annoyed right now," I say.

"Good thing you're over here then, huh?"

He slides easily into a song. On any given Friday night, an entire bar full of twenty-and-thirty-somethings can still sing every word to the handful of hits off The Devils & the Details's second album. That was the one that got them a little radio play and earned them the spots on those tour posters lining his wall. But it's still the covers that charm college kids into these local bars, and as such he knows them all: love ballads, sing-along songs, that earworm pop you hear on the radio. He runs through a few as easily as he runs his hands up my spine.

"You know Santa's going to bring you a bag of coal, right?" I retort. "Isn't that what you get when you're on the naughty list?"

"I found a workaround to that," he says. "I got you."

"Ha-ha. Tell me something I don't know."

"Like what?"

"Anything," I smile. "Everything."

His fingers move along the keys. Music fills the room, and the notes arrange themselves into an old Bowie song. His sidelong glance tugs at mine.

"There are eighty-eight keys on a piano. And eight is the symbol of infinity. And sometimes when I sit here I feel like I could make everything."

"And other times?"

"I feel like I'm a blip in time and space and that everything I do will always be nothing."

"Shit. Anything else I should know about you?"

"That I find that comforting?" he laughs. "That we're all just... accidentals. We fit, and we're here for a second, but the song never ends."

I let this sink in for a moment, into my heart and ribs and soul. I like him like this: lazy and late-night. I am just licking the crumbs of another poptart off my fingers when he transitions into that old familiar melody, the one I heard that very first night I became his neighbor. It soars and dances through the room, teasing through me before morphing into something else.

"Wait," I say. "What was that?"

"A song."

"Go back. I wanna hear the whole thing."

"Yeah, me too."

I give him a look, and he laughs. His hair falls across his face as he leans back into the music. Those bright eyes hold mine for a moment before pulling away.

"Seriously," I say. "I've heard you play it a hundred times.

There's got to be more to it."

"I agree that there is. Or that there should be. I just haven't finished it yet."

"Miles. It's been, like, three years."

Now it's his turn to give me a look.

"Some things take time, Cecilia."

Those words tingle through me. He's playing the piano intro to one of those songs about this very time of night, and it strikes a chord somehow, because it's not raining, and I'm not sleeping, but I'm also not lonely. His fingers are drawing out the verses when I settle across his lap, with my knees on either side of him. I'm kissing his neck, and he's sighing, and I'm smiling, because his notes are still mostly right, even though my robe has fallen open. I feel him already getting hard against me.

All I want for Christmas is for this to be real.

I don't even know if I know what that means, because clearly he's real. He's warmth and kissable skin and smirky smiles. He's music and magic and that slow-burn spark. He's kind and, yet, kind of still an asshole. He's also still my neighbor, but it's this feeling I want to last, like I want to spend the next fifty years – or at least the next five hours – wrapped up in him. Is that the late-night insanity taking over?

"What are you doing Christmas Eve?" he asks.

"This?" I murmur.

I hear him smile as I nibble at his ear.

"There's a concert. At St. Luke's. It's kind of a tradition thing. A few kids from my class are in it, and I always go. I want you to come."

It's the day after tomorrow, and the snow will probably be thawed by then, and I don't have any reason to say no. I drag my hand down his chest, kissing at his neck.

"Okay."

"Okay," he smiles.

When I bring my lips to his, he tastes like cinnamon. He doesn't lose the melody as he strings kisses across my shoulder, but in another moment I'm freeing him from those drawstring pants, and he's losing his breath.

"What are you doing?" he murmurs.

I kiss him again, and he bites my bottom lip, and he knows exactly what I'm doing. He's already hard, and I grip solid length of him. My robe is still slipping over my shoulders, and so is his concentration. I push back the bench and slide between his knees, and that look of wanting is everything. I take my time, revel in that shudder of breath as I run my tongue up the length of him, that low hum of pleasure as I let it slide across the contours of the hard, swollen tip. Testing. Teasing.

I know now why he was able to do this to me earlier – have control – because it's so fucking fun. And if I can't have him inside me, I want him like this. Sexy. Tortured. Looking at me like he might come before I even get him in my mouth. All those desperate breaths melt into a deep growl of a groan.

I lick him slowly, sinking into an innocent smile. "What do you wanna do?"

20.

By FOUR-THIRTY, we've devolved into entirely new ways to scandalize each other. And by this, I mean that I'm draped across his couch in a pair of his pajamas – which are way better than any that I own because men's pants have *pockets*, in case you haven't discovered this yet – and we're enjoying one of the great American pastimes of scrolling through streaming services for longer than it would take to watch an actual episode of something, and arguing about the merits of the options at hand.

"So you mean to tell me," I say, "that you've never seen *The Year Without a Santa Claus*."

"No," he laughs.

I narrow my eyes at him with the scrutinizing precision of someone who is just realizing she has a lot of serious work to do, as he lounges beside me with that perfectly messy hair and a look of amusement I find all too impossible.

"Heat Miser? Cold Miser?!"

"No," he says again.

I'm dancing around the room now, as if I've got a banded

boater hat and a backup crew of frosty minions, and I'm half-singing half-humming that famous tune about my clutch and how I'm too much.

"Wait, wait," he grins. "Maybe I know it. Can you do the dance again?"

I sink beside him, biting into my smile and snatching the remote away.

"No."

"Oh, c'mon. It's cute. It's like –"

He makes a sexy face and tries to flip his hand around like an imitation prop but just ends up convulsing with laughter against me. I elbow him upright.

"Okay then," I counter. "What's your must-have Christmas movie?"

When he finally catches his breath he says, "*A Christmas Carol.*"

"Which one?"

"What do you mean 'which one'?" he scoffs.

"I mean, there are a million versions of that, right?"

"Um, technically yes. But I'm talking about the only one that has ever mattered, which is the one that features Sir Patrick Stewart."

"Who?"

His face falls. "C'mon. Professor Charles Xavier. Captain Jean-Luc Picard. The voice of the CIA director in American Dad."

"Now you're just speaking words," I argue.

"This is," he laughs, shaking his head, "a complete injustice. An actual war on Christmas."

I shrug.

"Okay," he challenges, "which one do you like?"

"It's been a while. The Muppets one, maybe?"

"Oh god."

"Or that adaption with, what's his name, Bill Murray?"

"Don't even get me started on Bill Murray."

"What? Everyone likes Bill Murray."

"Do they, though? Or is it just one of those things that people like to say they like? Like Scarface. Or pumpkin beer."

My face is just a pressed line with raised eyebrows right now, because I swear he's not making any sense, but he cannot stop laughing.

"Any-*way*," he says, snatching the remote back from me. "I think this settles it. We've gotta watch them all."

"All what?"

"All the Christmas Carols. A Christmas Carol marathon."

"That'll take, like, a million hours."

"And after that million hours we can judge them on their merits."

I collapse against his chest. "Why do you do this to me?"

He grazes his lips across the edge of my smile. "Because you like it."

It's just that easy. It's a move, and a touch, and our kisses are greedy again. We tangle together, and he's pulling me on top of him, with his hands on my hips, and I can't get enough of that sound he makes when I move against him. He's groaning into my mouth, and grabbing at my ass, and god I wish I could fuck him just like this. I decide I will fuck him just like this, but not right now, unfortunately. I lick his lips before falling back onto my side of the couch, leaving him looking sexy and tortured.

"You're actually going to kill me," he sighs before sitting up.

We start the movie, and it's hard to pay attention, because he's sucking on my fingers and massaging my thighs and toying with my breasts.

"You're not watching," he says.

I sigh a little in response, and we are tangled up again. It goes on like this, through a few rounds of not-quite sex and a couple of half-watched movies, until daylight is hinting through the windows.

I can count the number of sunrises I've seen on one hand. Most of them were just a consequence of traveling, like when you get up before dawn to make that short trip to the airport or that long drive to the beach, but your mind is already somewhere else and you never really appreciate them. Not like this one, with its deep pink and light blue streaks of spun-cotton clouds.

When that first light breaks, I'm sitting beside him on our front steps, wrapped in blankets. The birds are already awake, and I'm watching our frosty breath and the heat rising off our cups of coffee. The city is still quiet, and there are only a few sets of tire tracks creased down the middle of the street, and I wonder if everyone else has decided to stay in bed. The frozen trees creak in the breeze like an old porch swing.

"We should go sledding," I say.

"You know at some point we have to sleep."

I scoff, and he laughs, and we're leaning into each other again, and he's nuzzling my cheek.

I've already been out traipsing around the yard in my boots and snapping pictures, and I don't know why, because it's not like the sun has never risen and people have never seen snow before, but for me, today feels... different. Magic. And I can't tell if it's the guy, or the endless staying-up-all-night sleepover exhaustion, but I'll take it.

"I like the way you look at things," he says.

He's watching me snag a shot of an especially round robin, with its red breast fluffed around its neck like a feathery scarf. I toss him a smile.

"How do I look at things?"

"I dunno. Like they're the most interesting things you've ever seen."

"Is that how I look at you?"

"Sometimes. When you're not looking at me like you want me to fuck off. Or fuck you."

That quiet thrill surges through me as I laugh, snapping his picture.

"How long have you been doing this?" he asks. "The photography, I mean."

I shrug. "Since high school, I guess. My aunt got me into it. It was kind of an inside joke. Every time she used to visit she would drag out all the photo albums, and we'd sit around the kitchen table, and I'd make her tell me the who and when and what and where of every single one. It was just a bunch of faded prints from them growing up in the seventies and old polaroids from me growing up in the nineties, but I dunno, I thought it was the coolest thing.

"So one year for my birthday she got me a camera, and she sent it with a big empty album and this note about how next time she visited she wanted us to sit around the kitchen table so I could tell her the whos and whats and whens and wheres of all the pictures I used to fill it up."

"And did you?"

"Yeah," I say, with the memory tugging at the corners of my mouth. "She got to see every bit of my angsty fifteen-year-old world."

"She sounds like a cool aunt."

"She is," I say, clicking one of the way the light glitters through the trees.

"So how did you get into weddings?"

"Money," I laugh. "Kidding. Sort of. I guess because they're those big album moments. Graduations, weddings, families, friends. That's the stuff people will look back on one day when they're, ya know, old and gray and sitting around their kitchen table. Or they'll use it as fuel for the burn-all-their-shit-in-a-fire-pit blaze of fury, after the divorce."

"And here I thought you were a romantic," he laughed.

I set up my camera down the front walk and jog back to the

steps where he is still wrapped up like a Sherpa. I shrug my blanket around my shoulders and scoot in beside him again.

"What are you doing?" he half-grins.

"Taking our picture. It's on a timer."

"You want a picture of this," he deadpans. "Twenty-four hours without sleep, sitting on the front porch, in pajamas."

"Yes. Now smile."

He is smiling, but he's not even remotely looking in the direction of the camera.

"You've got glitter on your face," he says.

"I've got glitter everywhere."

I drag my hands across the stubble of his jaw, kissing him. I breathe in the smell of coffee and cold and bite into my grin, because we are sparkling like the snow on the roofs, and I decide that falling in love has never been so easy. If that's what this is.

Love.

I'm not ready for it, but it's creeping in like the cold, and somewhere between all the laughing and dancing and snowfall, I think I fell.

"When you know you know," I could hear Joss saying.

And I don't know. I don't have a fucking clue. Because I can't think about anything except the way my heart flips when he looks at me like this, so I kiss him again, and again, until he's pulling me into his warmth and wrapping me in his arms, and it's the only place I want to be.

***

We've only been asleep for two hours when the phone rings. The room shifts as I stir, and I'm somehow more exhausted and delusional than if I never went to sleep at all. That obnoxious jingle is echoing through Miles's bedroom as dig through the pockets of my discarded robe. He's groaning and reaching for me across the blankets.

"Leave it," he mumbles.

"I can't," I say. "Baby watch."

But it isn't my mom calling. It's Eleanor. I rub my eyes, trying to bring the world into focus. She is the last person I expect to be calling, and there's a part of me that isn't sure if I should answer. There's another part, though, that can't connect the call quickly enough.

"Hello?"

"Cee?" she's sobbing.

"Eleanor," I say. "Ellie, what's wrong?"

"I, can't, do this," she hiccups.

"What?"

"This baby, won't, come out."

"Hey, no," I soothe. "Of course you can. Of course he will."

This doesn't elicit the desired response.

"Where's Robbie?"

"He went to find some food, and I'm so hungry, and I'm so tired, and --"

"Did you get any sleep?"

This isn't helping, and I sink to the edge of the bed, and she's sobbing again. I want to remind her that she's at a hospital, and that they should be able to just cut the thing out of her if this goes on too long, but that definitely seems like the wrong thing to say to a woman who's been in labor for over twelve hours, especially when you know she has spent the past nine months telling everyone who will listen about the miracle of "natural childbirth". I don't include any of this.

"Hey, listen to me," I say. "You're the strongest person I know. You can do this. And I know that sounds really cliché, probably, but it's the truth. I'm proud of you, Ellie. I'm so fucking proud of you. Do you hear me?"

I hear her suck in a breath.

"I miss you," she says. "I know you're mad at me, and I'm sorry, but I miss you."

"I know," I say, and I feel so shitty, and so helpless. "I'm sorry, too. I miss you, too. I'm not mad at you."

"You'd be so much better at this than me."

I laugh, but I've got tears in my eyes.

"That is a damn lie, and you know it. Remember that time you fell off the trampoline and broke your arm? I think I cried more than you did. Actually, I know I did."

She's laughing now, and it's a weak, mucousy sounding cough, but I'll take it.

"That's because you double-jumped," she says.

And now we're both laughing.

"Your baby is coming," I assure her. "And no matter how and when he gets here, he's gonna be beautiful. And I can't wait to be his aunt."

I hear my brother-in-law return to the room, and there's talk that they're going to let her eat something other than ice chips for breakfast, and she's not crying anymore, and I take my own shaky breath.

"Go meet our baby, okay?"

I put the phone on the bedside table and wipe my face, and I tell myself I'm good, that this is good, but the tears keep coming. I can't lie back down for fear that I'll drown, not only in my tears but in this feeling. Nobody ever tells you life can be this complicated, that in the same breath you can feel like your chest is a gaping hole that's been turned inside out and also that your heart can feel so happy and full. It's joy and pain and understanding and confusion, and it's doubling me over.

The thing about this grief is that I never felt like I deserved it. I didn't feel like I deserved for my body to catch me up in a cruel plot twist just as much as I felt like I didn't deserve to be upset about it, because Nate hadn't been upset, and we hadn't needed that baby, and in the end everything had fallen apart anyway. But it was mine, for a brief moment, and I can't explain how much it hurt, even if a part of me had made peace with it, and the world would say it was all for the best, and some days I would, too.

I feel the bed shift as Miles's fingers graze my back, and when I don't move to meet him, he draws himself up to sit beside me.

"Hey," he whispers. "It's okay."

He holds me against the soft-warm smell of his shoulder, and I'm the one sobbing now, and I can't really explain why, but he sits there until I curl across his lap and he's brushing tears off my face.

"It's okay."

He says it a hundred times like he hasn't said it once and would say it a hundred more. And somehow this – with my face blotchy and wet, and his forehead against my temple, and my heart filling and breaking – I know this is the very when.

21.

The city has been waiting for a proper snow day for so long that everyone seems to welcome this. It's not like Up North, where they have the special kind of tires to drive these roads and the infrastructure to clear away such things. Down Here, we welcome it as one of Mother Nature's permission slips: to stay inside, and slow down, and binge watch too much TV. The neighborhood businesses don't open. We hear tell of a twenty-four-hour gas station near the interstate that's operational, but it feels a lot like those mythical sanctuaries you see in post-apocalyptic movies, and we're not concerned enough to brave the elements and find out for ourselves.

Instead, we entertain ourselves by sleeping until three in the afternoon, and going out to admire the lopsided, two-foot tall snowman in the front yard a few houses down, and sticking a bottle of whiskey in the backyard to chill. Miles makes an Old Fashioned shortly after we wake up, and I'm finishing off his malbec and getting creative about what cocktails we can make with half a bottle of Kahlua, three fingers of vodka, and peppermint schnapps. Around five we shower, together, and at some points it's sexy, and at others I swear to him I'll never do it again because when he rinses his hair he acts like he's in a goddamn shampoo commercial and accidentally slings water in my face. Twice.

It's a perfect kind of day, that smells like fresh cold and tastes like orange bitters.

By seven, we're foraging for food. I'm arguing that the leftover casserole in my freezer is probably still fine, and he's telling me he'd maybe rather starve to death, and we're debating knocking over a Papa John's. Eventually, we consult Google and determine we can possibly make pizza. A sauceless, toppingless pizza. Okay, we can make cheesy bread. Maybe.

"Oh, you know what goes great with cheesy bread?" I say.

He alternates between kneading the dough and checking the instructions.

"A lot of stuff we don't have?"

"Yes," I admit. "But also, pineapple! I think I have some in my freezer!"

He is giving me a look like I've actually gone insane, but he waves me away with a flour-dusted hand like he knows I'm going to run over to my place and check anyway. And I am, one hundred percent. When I return with the frost-covered bag and a bonus jar of artichoke hearts, he looks even more concerned.

"You're gonna put fruit on our pizza," he says. "Frost-bitten fruit."

"It's not frost-bitten – I don't think. And it's not pizza." I swing myself up onto the counter and take a swig of my minty-rum drink. "Have you ever done this before?"

"Once," he says. "With Andrew. In high school. But there might have been marijuana involved."

"And you thought the pineapple was bad," I laugh.

"I'll admit, my mom was really pissed about the smell."

"Where is your mom this Christmas?"

He avoids my gaze for a moment, staring instead at the doughy lump we're hoping to turn into dinner.

"Las Vegas, I think. With what I assume is, by now, her fourth husband." He shrugs his eyebrows for emphasis. "It's kind of her Christmas tradition. Every few years or so she asks Santa for a new one."

"Oh," I offer. "They didn't invite you to the wedding?"

"I think weddings are pretty much the actual worst, so, no."

I gasp. "Weddings are not the worst. Usually. They're pretty. And romantic. And sweet."

"Samantha's weddings are not usually pretty, or romantic, or sweet," he smirks. "I think the last one involved a state penitentiary. But I'll take your word for it."

I match the name to that woman in her Margot Tenenbaum coat and Victoria's Secret perfume. His mom. The one who didn't recognize the place he'd been living for the past five plus years. The one who wasn't around when his grandfather was dying.

"I'm sorry."

"Really, don't be. She makes her own choices. Always has."

"So, who do you hang out with on Christmas?"

He points to Tom, who has knocked over our boots and is snoozing on them by the door. My chest clenches, and the feeling is at once endearing and heartbreaking.

"Well," I say, "he is my favorite neighbor."

"He is a pretty handsome motherfucker," he admits, glancing from me to Tom to the greased cookie sheet. "But I was hoping maybe I'd moved up in the ranks."

"I dunno. He hasn't forced me to watch five straight hours of *A Christmas Carol*."

"Hey, they call it a marathon for a reason. It requires endurance. And a willingness to take something way further than anyone with good sense would."

The way he looks at me makes me wonder the same thing Joss messaged me during our all-day nap: *Why haven't you banged him yet?*

Then, *You know the whole point of a holiday hookup is the actual hooking up.*

Followed by, *Is this that celibacy nonsense again?*

No, I replied.

Not that she was that much more understanding of my actual explanation. She had long since been a big fan of the pull-out philosophy and had wasted no time sending me an article from Gloss about its widespread popularity and effectiveness.

And believe me, I thought about it. But I had also thought about that diagram they'd shown us in high school health class, where they connected a bunch of cartoon people with red strings to the one sad sack standing in the middle like Patient Zero. I just happened to be the only obsessive germaphobe who actually took the lesson to heart. More than that, there was also something akin to Nate's parting words swimming in my head.

You do you, boo, she said. *But please know that you deserve sex. Mind-blowing, guilt-free, just-because-you-feel-like-it sex.*

Maybe tomorrow, I sent back.

Good, because I kind of wanna know what all the fuss is about.

I sent her a side eye, and she closed the conversation with a kissy face.

"Any word on your sister?" he asks.

"She has officially been in labor for twenty-four hours. But based on the last update, it should be any time now. Speaking of which, I should really go next door and grab my charger."

"Really?" he says, shooting me an incredulous look. "This again? Don't you remember what happened last time?"

I laugh in spite of myself. "I think that was a one-time thing."

"Fine," he says. "I think I might have one in my bedroom, though."

His hands are still coated in oil and dough, and I slide off the counter.

"Whereabouts?" I ask.

"Um, top desk drawer, maybe?"

I swing into the room, where we left the comforter in a tangle that is sliding off onto the floor. I'm already thinking about how I would feel better if I made it, with the pillows fluffed and the corners tucked in, when I open the desk drawer and find the charger. And the square black packaging with a Greek warrior on the front.

A small laugh escapes me, and I'm just about to march back into the kitchen triumphantly, when a feeling sneaks through me that isn't exactly triumphant. The box is open, and I have a feeling, given the proximity to his bed, that maybe it always resides here. That last night, when we were rummaging through his bathroom cabinets, he would've known to check here. And for some reason, he didn't. My face grows hot and tingly.

"Did you find it?" he calls.

"Yeah," I say.

When I walk back into the kitchen, my throat feels tight. He's sliding the baking sheet into the oven.

"All right," he announces. "Fifteen minutes."

He picks up his drink, but it only takes a second for his smile to falter. I want to be wrong. When his gaze drops to that little black box I've placed on the counter, I know for sure that I'm not.

I try to keep a lightness in my voice when I say, "Found these, too."

"Awesome," he nods, but it's one of those moments when it's not what someone says but how he says it. With a pause. A hesitation. And it makes the confusion burn across my face even more, because this is just *weird.*

"I think I'm gonna go."

And somehow it stings even more that he isn't trying to explain this away. It's not really a question of if he wants me, but why he doesn't want me like that. If I were any other girl, I'd already have become a member of that not-so-selective club, and that alone makes me feel both insulted and stupid, because a) how am I not good enough to be one of those girls and b) why the hell did I ever think I wanted to be?

And if there's something else, like maybe he made his own celibacy vow, or he's trying to turn over a new leaf, or he just wanted to wait, then he could've just told me, and that would have been fine. But he didn't, and he knows me, and he knew I wouldn't have anything at my place, and he knew the stores were all closed, and given the events of the past year, he would have had a pretty good idea about my stance on the importance of contraceptives, and all this just feels like a plan that I'm not privy to.

And god, what if this is also about that? That he believes I am that girl who is desperately trying to trick some guy into making a baby? That seems like an absolutely insane thing to think, but he's not giving me a whole lot else to work with.

"Yeah, okay," he offers.

There's a resignation in his voice, and I feel too foolish to keep standing here, so I nod. I shrug into my coat and rouse sleeping Tom from my boots. The kitchen feels too hot, and the air outside feels too cold, and in between those two realizations he's got so much time to say anything. But he doesn't. He leans against the counter with his arms folded over his cable-knit chest, and he lets me walk right out the door.

22.

Even though the first pictures of baby Silas Maxwell Broslin are of him slimy and pink and screaming, I swear he's one of the most beautiful things I've ever seen. Slightly amphibious-looking, yes. But tucked against Eleanor's sweaty, tear-streaked smile? Abso-fucking-lutely beautiful.

I always hate how people swoon and swear that infants look like this relative or that, because they always sort of look like baby geckos to me, but in the pictures, I really think he looks like Ellie, with his headful of dark hair and his pouty, Gerber-baby mouth. My dad sends me a million of them, and my mom facetimes me, and in the quiet cold of my apartment I almost feel like I'm there. As soon as this snow melts, I swear I will be.

I don't know why I'm still awake, but it's not because of any after-midnight piano songs. I haven't heard a sound since I retreated back to my side of the world. Not music, not his front door, not the groan of the pipes when he showers or shaves. Part of me is relieved, but the rest of me wishes he would play something loud and annoying, like this silence is too much.

I think about going back over there a hundred times. I think about demanding an explanation. I think about pretending it didn't bother me and calling a truce. I think about how I'd much rather be eating that cheesy bread than a bowl of plain white rice, which tastes so much like nothing that it could almost taste like anything, except for the dinner I'm missing out on. I puzzle through a hundred scenarios, but my brain is suffering from thirty-two hours of too much booze and too little rest.

Even still, I imagine he's knocking on my door, looking just as desperate as I feel, and pulling me into him, until we're that insatiable press of lips and skin and heat. In another version, I'm falling through his doorway, and our clothes are coming off again, and we're getting each other off again. But in most of these imagined scenarios, we're just laughing on his couch, with my legs across his lap, pretending we never did anything more, because maybe that's the easiest piece with us, the part where he could almost be my friend.

I want to call Joss, but I know she's asleep, and even though she wouldn't mind waking up, I also know she's currently sharing a room with her two eight-year-old cousins, and I have a feeling nobody wants them woken up. This isn't really a text message conversation. I actually don't know what this is. Not words, really, but an unidentifiable feeling. It's not like I think she could fix it, but I hope she would understand.

I'm wrapped in too many layers to consider pulling myself off the couch, and I click through the endless movie options on my TV, pausing on the list of holiday favorites. I see one of the many Dickens adaptations lurking right there at the edge of the screen. I scroll over and check the cast. It's the one we were saving for the very end, with Patrick Stewart. I double back to the menu and consider watching Love Actually for the millionth time. I even start it, but somewhere in the first fifteen minutes I back out, and I find *A Christmas Carol* again and hit play.

He wasn't kidding. It really is the best one.

***

Is this what a one-night stand feels like?

This uneasiness that is part-despair, part-dread, that swarms in my head like a bad hangover as I walk the slushy sidewalk to Matilda's. The midday sun has warmed things up a bit, and a few cars have braved it. One of them is stuck in the middle of the intersection, and the tires spin endlessly as the light turns from green, to yellow, to red. Three people are currently slipping around out there, trying to push it to a point it can regain traction. I don't miss that it's the same cross-street where we left those snow angels, which have long since been filled in and tracked over, and I feel like it's an apt metaphor, really. They lasted about as long as we did.

Why the hell do people do this for fun?

I mean, besides all that fun we did actually have, before we suddenly didn't.

In the burgers-and-fries warmth of the restaurant, I find Cat Glasses and Fabulous Fedora sitting at the bar and slide in next to them.

"It's not the ice storm of '94," she offers. "But it is a lot more than we expected, huh?"

"Infinitely," I say.

"Did you manage to stay warm, at least?"

There's no innuendo in her tone, and I know she means about the power lines not having frozen, but I'm distracted by the fuzzy memory of them joking about body heat, and the not-so-fuzzy memory of Miles kissing my neck.

"Oh yeah," I say. "Although my furnace leaves a lot to be desired. And my fridge was definitely not full enough for this."

I order a bowl of tomato soup and a grilled cheese, hoping it will help soak up all the regret.

Carmen is behind the bar today. She's probably old enough to be someone's grandmother, but she's rocking purple hair, a hoop in her nose, and a low-cut top that shows off her ample chest. She brings me a big glass of water with a maternal nod that says she knows I haven't had enough of it over the past couple of days.

"And would you like a side of aspirin with that?"

"That bad?" I grimace, wondering if I should have used more concealer. "I showered and everything."

"You've got a hickey on your neck and glitter on your forehead."

They all give me a look.

"Strip club?" Fabulous Fedora inquires.

"Snowball fight," I reply.

"Sure thing," Carmen guffaws before sweeping my menu away.

I'm laughing in spite of myself, because it does sound like a poorly thought-out cover. I take a few gulps of water, wondering if I can drown out the reality.

"Big plans for Christmas?" Cat Glasses asks.

I think about how I told Miles I'd come to the concert at St. Luke's. It's only a couple of blocks over, and I know a lot of the neighborhood usually goes. Somehow blowing him off over something that I promised right before I blew him makes me feel like a real jerk. I don't offer up any of this.

"I might drive up to Nashville, if the roads clear. My nephew was born this morning," I smile.

"Congratulations!" they say. She adds, "Are you an aunt, auntie, or one of those modern things?"

"Modern things like what?"

"Ti-ti. Ni-ni. Cee-cee."

"I actually haven't decided yet. But Cee-cee does have a nice ring to it."

I show them the pictures on my phone, and they coo over him accordingly.

"A Christmas baby," Cat Glasses swoons.

"Fun for us," I agree. "Probably less fun for the poor kid who has to almost share his birthday with Jesus."

"Oh, that's an easy fix. Haven't you ever heard of Christmas in July? You'll be his favorite aunt."

"Well I better be. I'm his only aunt," I smile. "What about you guys? Any plans?"

"We usually have a potluck with some friends, but this year, who even knows. It might just be us and a whole party platter of peppermint bark."

I consider that this doesn't sound half bad. We glance at the sound of the open door, which brings with it the screechy vroom of those still-stuck tires out in the street, and also, inexplicably, the last couple on earth I ever want to see again.

He's wearing what I recognize as the only plaid button down he owns, rolled up to his forearms even though it's still literally freezing outside. She's a waif in a retro, knee-length, multi-colored coat, and even in that gray knit hat I know it's her. His hand finds her lower back as he ushers them inside. I turn around, hoping they don't see me, or that if they do, they at least have the decency to pretend otherwise. Carmen, however, notices.

"Isn't that that guy you used to –"

"Yes," I say.

"Do you want me to kick him out?"

I love that she would do that for me, but I shake my head. "Just my lunch to-go, if that's okay?"

"Sure thing."

He and Pixie Cut take our old booth, and I realize she must live near here. It's highly likely he went to her place after I kicked him out of mine. What are the fucking odds?

I want to crawl out of my skin, and some part of me can't get out of here fast enough. Then I hear Miles's voice in my head, from when we were out front, shivering on the sidewalk.

"Are you really going to let him run you out of your own bar?"

He's not even here, and he's still right.

"Hey, Carmen," I say. "Nevermind. I'm hanging out for a bit."

Her mouth quirks into a smile, and she gives me a knowing nod.

It's not a huge triumph, in the grand scheme of things. I don't march over and cause a big scene. I don't tell my cohorts, loud enough for Pixie Cut to hear, about the ex I found in my bed the night before and all the awful things he said. I don't even throw them searing, sidelong glances. All I do is sit on a barstool, weigh in on a debate over Pancho's cheese dip versus Rotel, and eat my lunch like it's any other day. But it feels like a victory, because this time, he isn't even remotely looking at me like I might take him home. He isn't looking at me at all.

"I would've killed him," Joss will tell me later, and part of me will agree. Somewhere, though, between the last time I was sitting in this bar and now, I realized that he's the one who has to live with himself, and I'm just really glad that I don't. Not anymore.

***

I use the late afternoon to catch up on some work. Maybe it's a holiday for most, but not for me. These are the moments when my obsessive planning keeps me level – and paid. Across town there's a couple waiting for their engagement photos, and I've got a wedding booked on New Year's, which will easily consume my next few weeks, so this project deserves some love, even though it's Christmas Eve. It's not like I've got much else to do.

I retrieve one of the chocolate chip cookies that Carmen bagged up for me, turn on some holiday tunes, and cycle through the shots. Despite the potential of the raw images, I can easily spend hours in edits. The perfectionist in me can somehow see the difference between every little level of brightness or color or contrast, and adjusting it all is like piecing together a puzzle for which there could be a million configurations. I'm always looking for the one that is going to make this not just another picture but *the* picture. The picture they share with their friends, the picture they place on their mantel, and yes, maybe even the picture they one day show their nieces or nephews or kids.

In the best one of the bunch, the fountain is winter-magic sparkly behind them, and they are silhouetted by those frosty fairy lights. He's down on one knee, and she's got her hands pressed against her mouth, but her eyes say it all: that this moment is unbelievable in all the best ways.

I adjust it so her red scarf pops, in a long sweep out behind her, because it has just been caught by the breeze, even though the two of them are caught up in the stillness between breaths. How I snagged this after sneaking out of the bushes I will never quite understand, but maybe that's the reason it's my favorite. They were so caught up in each other that they barely noticed me.

It's already dark when I work my way through the last of them, and I get up to click on a lamp. It's six-thirty, and it is apparent I'm probably just having cookies for dinner as I sink back into my chair. I'm saving the first draft of the project when I stumble into those next images that are white with snow.

String lights. Quiet streets. Misty frost among the hazy-dark trees.

Miles.

Me.

Our two messy snow angels, lying in the street.

I've been running all of this through my mind so much the past couple of days that I almost feel like I've seen them all already, and I'm about to click out of the folder when I see us sitting on the front porch. The snow is soft, and the sky is streaked with light, and we are smiling into each other. Like the camera doesn't exist. Like nothing exists, actually, except this moment, that is unbelievable in all the best ways. It tugs straight through me.

I sigh.

He told me once that I'm the girl who cares too much what everything looks like. I am, it's true. But with those pictures blown up on my screen, I know exactly what this looks like. Why then, am I still assuming the worst of him?

My blood quickens in my veins, and I chew the inside of my lip in indecision. It's six forty-five. I'm already dressed, my apartment is cold, and if I leave right now, maybe I won't be too late. The moment stretches across one breath, two, three. My mind races through possibilities. There are so many ways this could go, and too many things this could mean, but I acknowledge that none of them are going to happen from my couch. I tug on my boots, snug into my scarf, and slip out into the snow.

23.

If there's any magic left in the world, it is here in the candlelight hush of this church. The wood and marble details greet me past the stone steps. Even from the entryway, the choir sounds like a chorus of cherub angels, and it reminds me of all those Christmases as a kid when my grandmother would visit. I'm taking off my hat and crossing myself as I slip into the sanctuary, just like I used to, even though I'm many years removed from that girl and probably half as hopeful. Most of my conversations with God this year have been angry rants and desperate pleas, and yet, this place feels so inviting.

An attendant greets me with a white taper and motions me to one of the many empty spaces near the middle, but I slide onto a wooden pew near the back, not because I'm trying to hide but because it has the best view of the entire scene. It's been a long time since I've been in a church for anything other than a wedding, and without the nervous-looking grooms and the bridesmaid processionals, the details feel different. The hanging chandeliers are darker, and the setting more intimate. Christmas trees are crowded onto either side of the stage like an evergreen forest, and the whole place smells of fir and pine and incense.

Up on the stage, the collection of pre-teens are in their Sunday best, and they're singing with a somber seriousness that I find endearing. I recognize the hymn as one of my grandmother's favorites, and my chest fills with nostalgia as the sopranos sweep across the chorus. The rows in front of me are scattered with parents, teachers, and parishioners, each of them looking just as enchanted, and the place feels so full that I almost forget that I'm sitting alone.

A few minutes later, someone scoots in beside me. Miles. There's a tie peeking above the collar of tonight's sweater. He motions to my unlit candle with his. I reluctantly oblige, holding still until the flames catch.

"You came," he whispers.

I realize in the time it took me to walk over here, I hadn't really considered what we might say to each other. I actually wasn't even sure if I would see him here, but now he's sitting right here, and I'm acutely aware of the small space between my shoulder and his.

"I said I would," I say. "And unlike you, I value honesty."

He sighs. "Cecilia."

"Sh," I warn.

He glances around, but nobody is looking our way. Our voices are completely hidden under the boastful thrum of the organ and the candor of the choir.

"I did – do – want to have sex with you," he whispers.

I glare at him, incredulous, and possibly more scandalized by this than I should be. "I don't think you're supposed to say 'sex' in a church."

"What am I supposed to say then? That I want to 'lay' with you, in the biblical sense?"

"God, no," I grimace. "I don't want to talk about this. Really."

"Then why are you here?"

Someone is glancing over now, a white-haired lady who looks like she is ready to send us both to detention. Miles straightens, glancing at the dancing flame in his hands. His question, however, is a valid one. Unfortunately, I don't really have an answer for it.

"Can't we just... call a truce?" I ask.

He's giving me one of those probing, unreadable looks now, and I almost think he's going to accept, but he surprises me by shaking his head. I have no idea what this means. I roll my eyes. I think about getting up, heading home, but I remember that it's Christmas. The church is warm, the music is lovely, and I don't want to spend the night alone in my apartment. I'm hemmed into this pew, anyway. So I stay.

"I don't want to fight with you," I whisper.

"Are those my only options?"

I cut my gaze at him. When I sigh, the flame flickers in front of me. We grow quiet again. A tiny little soprano in a green, silky dress steps up to the front of the group, and Miles's smile takes on a hint of pride.

"Paloma," he offers. "One of my sixth graders."

Her voice is ten times bigger than she is, but delicate, and haunting, as it scales over the Latin lyrics of a tune I recognize as "O Come All Ye Faithful". The rest of the voices fade in, growing and overlapping until the sound is so delightful and surprising that I can't help but smile.

"She's really something."

"I can't take any credit," he admits. "But I have a feeling one day I'll be telling them that on an episode of *Behind the Music*."

He points out a few more of his, like an admiring big brother. There's David, who is about two heads taller than the rest of his classmates and looking particularly awkward about it, and Skyler, who keeps tugging the long braid of the alto in front of him, who is also named Skyler. She imperceptibly steps on his toes at one point. I'm fighting a laugh when I wonder if they're going to stop singing and transition into an outright scuffle. Both fortunately and unfortunately, that doesn't happen. But one kid we don't know does sneeze so violently during "Gloria in excelsis Deo" that he blows out the two candles nearest him and the next five minutes look like a Monty Python skit of an attendant trying, unsuccessfully, to relight them.

I can see, though, why so many in the neighborhood come here every year, especially since afterwards they serve food. After the show, when we drift into the entryway, the savory smell of it is wafting down the hall. I'm not planning to stay for it. Miles is fielding greetings from half the people who pass us, and I feel like I should leave before things get awkward, because I'm not his girlfriend, or really his date, or even his one-night stand. The resignation has already settled into my limbs. There is nothing between us that can't be easily forgotten. Or at least, easily ignored until one of us finally moves.

I notice all the ways he's not touching me as he comes back over. He's running a nervous hand through his hair, like he notices it, too, and I'm already trying to make my excuses, when Liv Dennison sweeps up and gives us a matching set of perfume-scented hugs.

"Your kids were just magnificent this year," she tells him. "Just like you and Andrew used to be up there. Well, maybe more you than Andrew. I think he was just in it for the girls."

"It's middle school," Miles says. "I think all the guys are in it for the girls."

I'm watching him now. Maybe more than the poptarts, or the parties, this is more his Christmas tradition than anything else. And he invited me. Of course, that was before I knew he was secretly trying not to have sex with me, but that tingly feeling warms my chest like whiskey anyway. He sees me looking and just shrugs his eyebrows at me.

"C'mon," she says, hooking her arms through ours. "Let's get a drink."

"I should really get home," I begin.

"Nonsense," she says. "Flynn already found us a table."

Resistance, somehow, seems futile. We follow the flow of the crowd into the small reception hall, where they're serving holiday ham and festive hors d'oeuvres, and it almost surprises me to find that there isn't a woman waiting in a long white dress. I actually think I've shot a few weddings here.

The kids have already swarmed through the buffet line and taken over a few rowdy tables, but Flynn is waiting for us at one by the window.

"Darling, you remember Cecilia?"

I don't know why he would, but he's pretty convincing as he comes to his feet and shakes my hand.

"Of course! Merry Christmas," he says. "Please, have a seat. I'll grab us all some drinks. What are you having?"

"Oh, I'm really not staying long," I start again.

"Just a small glass then," he says, and I laugh in spite of myself. Miles gets up to grab us a few plates of food, and Liv settles into her seat confidentially.

"So, how long have you been seeing Miles?"

"Oh. We're not really... He's just my... We're neighbors."

"Oh, I misunderstood," she apologizes. "I guess I should have known, after the mistletoe. Sorry about that, by the way. I blame my in-laws. They met under the mistletoe in 1959, if you can believe it. Which I do not. I'm pretty sure they met at a VFW, but I guess that doesn't make as good of a story."

"I guess not," I laugh.

"So you live in Tom's old place then?"

I blink for a moment, not understanding. "Tom, as in... Major Tom?"

She laughs. "No, no, sorry. Human Tom. Miles's grandfather."

Something in me stills, but my brain is trying to process too many things at once.

"I, um... yeah, I guess so," I offer. "He hasn't really talked about it. That's weird, isn't it, to have a human Tom and a cat Tom?"

"He named Major Tom after himself," she laughs. "Tom always had a funny sense of humor. He's the reason Miles moved back, you know. He wouldn't say it – said he got tired of the road, and maybe that's true, too – but when the cancer came back, there he was. But it makes sense. Tom practically raised him."

Suddenly, I understand why Major Tom sometimes lingers outside my back door or jets into my place. I understand why Miles's mom got confused about the apartments. I even get, on some level, why he never moved.

"That's funny," I offer, "because he said the same thing about you."

"Me? No," she scoffs. "He's too sweet, that boy. I think of him as one of my own, but Tom was his role model. A real gentleman. And not a bad pianist, either. I half-expected Miles to head back out on the road when he died, but I'm glad he didn't. I think this life suits him."

She smiles across the room now, where Miles has been accosted by his students. One of the Skylers has dragged him to what is clearly the guys' table, and Miles listens as they talk emphatically, each one competing to tell whatever it is that needs telling, the way kids do. Then I smile, too, because Miles gives David a fist bump, and the painfully awkward kid looks like he couldn't feel more cool.

"Yeah," I say. "Maybe so."

I'm trying to imagine him, now, as a gentleman. To see him through that lens, not as the indie frontman with the crooked smile who leaves a trail of broken hearts behind him, but as the teacher, and the mentor, and the guy who, at thirty, still won't address his best friend's parents without sticking a mister or missus in front of their names.

Flynn returns with our snacks and drinks.

"You're not telling her a bunch of embarrassing stories about him, are you?" he asks. "She always swears she's not going to do it and then ends up spilling everyone's secrets."

"I do not!" she protests.

"She does," he mouths to me, as she's shaking her head. "The boys won't let her talk to their dates without a chaperone."

"Well now I've got to hear one. Or several," I say, not even bothering to remind them that I'm not his date.

"Oh, I dunno. He was always so much more behaved than my boys."

Miles expertly navigates the parade of family members between the kids' tables and ours and sinks into the seat beside me as if on cue. He notes the way everyone is smiling and then glances around the table nervously.

"Oh god, you're not telling her anything embarrassing are you?"

She opens her mouth in mock offense.

"You two are in cahoots, aren't you?" she laughs, eyeing her husband.

"Well," Miles counters, "two can play this game. Did she happen to tell you about the time she signed me and Andrew up for etiquette classes?"

"Etiquette classes?" I question.

"Like a bad adaptation of a Jane Austen novel. Preening. Prancing. Weird waltzy-dancing."

"Oh, it wasn't that bad," she insists. "But if you're going to bring that up you should also include how you both got kicked out on the third day."

"I still don't know which of those bajillion forks to use. It's been bothering me for years."

"Wait, wait," I laugh. "Kicked out for what?"

"A combination of things," he says.

Liv, whose expression says she cannot let his nonchalance stand, adds, "The culmination of which was drawing penises on all the placecards at the luncheon table."

I shoot him a disappointed look.

"We were thirteen," he defends.

"Boys," she sighs. "If I had a dollar for every time one of them drew a damn penis on something."

"Trust me, as a middle school teacher, I'm doing my penance."

"And I'm very proud of you," she says. "Your grandfather would be, too."

Flynn raises a toast, and we all drink to it, even though it leaves Miles looking uncharacteristically sheepish. He glances over, giving me an imperceptible little shrug, like it's nothing, but somehow I can tell that it has meant the world to him, and with the way Liv is smiling, I know she knows it, too.

She says it again before we leave, pulling him into one of her cheek-kissing hugs. She smudges at the lipstick print with her thumb. She wraps me in her perfume-scented arms as well, squeezing me for just a second, like she's punctuating the moment.

"You kids be good, okay?" she says.

"No promises," he smiles.

And I realize this must be one of their things, and it wraps around my heart until I'm smiling, too. They leave, encouraging him to come over tomorrow, but I think we all know for some reason he won't.

We linger in front of the wreath-clad doors of the church. The stained glass looms above us, bright and reminiscent of a colorful kaleidoscope, casting intricate shadows across the snow. He's got his collar turned up, and his hands in his pockets, and when he looks at me, he's got that same quiet resignation, like he knows that nothing has changed. And yet, maybe he's feeling hopeful.

"Walk you home?" he says.

I think about saying no, that it isn't a good idea, because we really can't do this. Me and him. As much as I kind of want to. It's been a bad idea from the start, and I know I'm overthinking it the way I always do, but I don't need a cipher to know that he let me walk away for a reason. Despite all this, we're going the same direction, so I nod.

We head down the thawing sidewalk in silence. A few cars creep by, and with the increase in traffic the main streets are looking gray and dirty. All of the magic of the past few days is melting into soggy puddles. I tug my coat more tightly around me against the cold. I think, a few times, that he's going to launch into the explanation he'd been trying to offer me in the church, but he doesn't. Maybe it's because I told him not to, even though that was a lie. I do want to talk about it. Or rather, I want to know. I guess I am hoping to absorb the truth like osmosis without actually having to say anything.

By the time we make it to our front walk, we haven't said a word. I'm already mentally preparing myself to tell him goodnight and retreat inside my place. His silence says it all, doesn't it? And I don't want to drag this out, when it's clear neither of us knows where we want it to go.

Maybe this is why I don't notice the icy patch on the steps, where the melting snow has refrozen with the nightfall. In a slow-motion instant, my boot loses traction. I slip, I scream, and suddenly I'm falling – directly into him. If this were a movie, I think he would catch me in a graceful way, and we would lock eyes, and he'd pull me into a kiss. But this is not a movie, so when he reaches for my flailing form, I knock him square in the face, and we slide to the slushy sidewalk in a cascade of curses. Pain shoots through my hip.

"What the hell," I groan.

"Real graceful," he grumbles.

I am wet, and cold, and dazed as we untangle ourselves. He is gaping into nothingness, trying to blink away the stunned look on his face. I sit up, brushing the ice off of me. The skin beneath his eye already looks swollen and red.

"You couldn't have caught me?" I ask.

"Not when you're flopping around like that."

"I was not flopping, I was *falling*."

"Same thing," he says, bringing a hand to his head. "Fuck."

I draw closer, trying to make sure he isn't bleeding or concussed. Not that I know how to diagnose a concussion. Given the way my elbow is throbbing, though, I must have hit him pretty hard.

"Does it hurt?"

I touch it tentatively, and he winces, pulling away.

"It hurts more when you poke it like that."

"I'm sorry," I say again. "There's ice on the steps."

"No shit," he offers.

For some reason, we both start laughing. The frustration between us softens. I carefully drag myself to my feet before offering him a hand. He's holding his head as he stands.

"Do you still have that first aid kit?" I ask.

"I'm fine," he insists.

"Maybe I meant for me."

He knows I didn't, but he lets us into his place anyway. I follow him into the vintage tile confines of his bathroom, and he perches against the edge of the sink while I inspect him in the light. The knot is already trying to bruise. I prod around it again, more carefully this time.

"Swelling is a good sign, right?"

He's watching me warily. "I think it's a sign you elbowed me in the face."

There's teasing in his voice, and when I smile that gaze dips across my mouth. It's only a flicker of a moment, but it's enough to make my heart tumble around in my chest the way I fell down those stairs.

"I think you're fine," I offer.

I should go.

The moment is already magnetic, and that look holds me close. He's running his hand down my arm, and this is a bad idea, because we've been here before. Maybe I can blame it on muscle memory, the way I find myself leaning in.

"I thought you didn't," I murmur, "want to", but my words are lost in his lips.

He grazes his mouth against mine. In a single sigh I'm against his chest, and his hands are framing my face, pulling me in deeper.

"I thought you didn't want to talk about it."

And he's right, I don't want to talk. We're already cold hands against warm skin, and even as we're taking off my dress I know this doesn't make any sense. I tug at his tie until his groan meets my lips, and I'm so glad I wore the sexy, thigh-high tights, and I don't even care if they make it look like I planned this, because he's squeezing my ass, and biting kisses across my bare shoulder, and I'm undoing his belt. The sound of him losing his breath aches through me, and I pull him closer.

"Please," I breathe.

This isn't graceful. Our hands are greedy and our breath is impatient and the way I want him is already pounding through me. We stumble into the next room and fall into his bed. And he knows exactly what I meant, but he's moving against me, and breathing words across my neck.

"Please what?"

I groan, grabbing handfuls of his hair. "Oh my god seriously. I just need you to fuck me."

I know how I mean it. That is not how it comes out. Which makes it absolutely the wrong thing to say. I realize this a beat too late.

In a breath he's pulling away from me, and rolling onto his back, and sighing his hands across his face.

"We can't do this."

My body is still aching, but my head is muddled with confusion, and I kind of want to elbow him in the face – on purpose, this time.

"What the actual fuck?" I say.

I'm sitting all the way up now, shocked and annoyed and feeling stupid. He's straining against his boxers, and I know he wants to, and clearly I want to, and I just don't understand why this has to be so hard.

"What is the problem, Miles?" I'm already getting up, snatching my clothes off the floor. "If I was any other girl --"

"Is that what you really want, Cecilia? You want to be any other girl? You want me to fuck you and forget about you?"

My face is hot, and I still don't understand, but I'm angry.

"Oh, fuck you. Don't act like you're so morally superior, all the sudden. Like you're trying to spare me from some sort of cock amnesia. Like you haven't done this a hundred fucking times."

He's laughing now, a frustrated, humorless sound.

"I knew when I saw you sitting at the bar that you just wanted someone – anyone – and this is my fault, too, but I can't be your revenge fuck, or your pity fuck, or someone you sleep with when you're feeling too fucking sorry for yourself."

My eyes are stinging with tears now as I glare at him.

"This is my fault?" I demand. "Ha, okay. Why? Because you're, like, in love with me or something?"

The blow lands just how I mean for it to, but I immediately regret it. He's pulling up his pants and brushing past me into the bathroom.

"You can tell everyone we did it, if it'll make you feel better."

He tosses the rest of my clothes at me and doesn't look back as he continues getting dressed. I pull them on with blurred vision and I'm so embarrassed, and hurt, and downright pissed, but I refuse to fucking cry, because this is too ridiculous. I step into the chill of my apartment with tears streaming down my face anyway.

Because I could've just never left the bar with him.

And I could've just never come back to his place.

Or I could've just told him the truth.

24.

I'M ON THE ROAD BEFORE THE SUN COMES UP ON CHRISTMAS MORNING. The only sign that it snowed is the frost clinging to the grass and dusting across the trees, but the temperatures are climbing back into the fifties, as they do in the South. Once I'm half an hour north there's no hint of ice at all. There isn't much traffic, given that it's a holiday, and it's just me and a few eighteen-wheeler trucks traveling up the interstate. Long drives have always helped me clear my head, giving me the sense of going somewhere when my thoughts feel stuck-still, and I need this one. The fact that I'm going to meet my nephew is an added bonus.

Around the second hour, Joss calls and I bring her up to speed on the whole crazy thing. I tell her about the traditional holiday party, drag her through the snow, describe how I'm beyond done with Nate, and even throw in a few dirty details, including that rooftop kiss I had previously left out.

"Wait, you did what? When?"

"Halloween," I sigh.

"I'm going to forgive you for this," she interjects, "only because I need to hear the whole thing. And what's a cravat?"

I tell her about the smudged whiskers, and the Latin dancing, and the stupid snow angels. My entire retelling is nonsensical, I'm sure, broken up into bits and pieces and shuffled out of order, but she punctuates it with the appropriate commentary and occasional snort. When I'm done, the car fills with the hum of my tires and radio silence. Along the hilly slopes beside the interstate, the spindly trees look like witches' fingers, rising up into the misty morning. Endless gray stretches out in front of me.

"Say something," I finally prompt.

"Well. He's either fucked in the head, or he's completely in love with you. Possibly both."

"Not helpful."

"Sorry," she says. "But like, is this really so bad? It doesn't sound like he's asking you to sign a ten-year contract or anything. Just that he wants you to want him."

"Now you just sound like an '80s song."

"For more than just the sex," she adds with a chortle. "To, ya know, maybe take out on dates and have a real shot with, outside of the Bermuda triangle of the trifecta."

I chew the inside of my lip and merge lanes. She has a point. Regardless of whether you call it the Bermuda triangle or the snowglobe effect, there was certainly a suspended animation aspect to it. Something a bit surreal. I think about what he said to me that night when the world was still a winter wonderland.

"Has it ever occurred to you that they were using me?"

My face heats, and I wonder if that's how I looked to him. Actually, I know it is, after our most recent conversation. Which is probably fine for someone you don't care about, but not exactly what you want from a girl you've secretly been carrying a torch for since the night you met. But no. The sex wouldn't have ruined anything, at least no more than we had currently managed to ruin everything. Then again, maybe it would have. Maybe the snow would've thawed and things would've gone exactly how they did on that rooftop.

"This never happened."

If I changed the lens, I could read that look on his face now. Like I'd played him as the fool. All this time I thought he was the asshole. Maybe, from his perspective, it had also been me.

"I think you like him."

I watch the road rising into the hills, and the white lines guiding me along. I wonder if I could drive forever, straight across the country and into the ocean, so I wouldn't have to face up to the way I felt when I was dancing with him in the street, and arguing with him on the couch, and eating poptarts with him in his kitchen. The prospect somehow seems easier than dealing with all of these feelings. I wonder, as I always do, why the truth has to hit so fucking hard. Eventually, I sigh.

"Yeah," I admit. "I think I do, too."

***

Silas is more perfect in person than I could ever imagine. I hold him in my arms and pace around Ellie's hospital bed on my road-weary legs. She's watching me like this is Christmas morning and she's opening the best gift she ever received, again and again. I've never held anything so gently and yet with so much focus, like I'm terrified I might drop him, even though he's only six pounds, and I've probably got cameras heavier than he is.

"Oh, hey," I sigh. "Happy birthday, little guy."

He stretches his mouth with a squawk and squeezes his teensy hand around mine. Is this where that saying comes from, about being wrapped around someone's finger? His hair is a downy little mohawk, and his eyes are a searching, nondescript hazel, and in that moment he's got my whole damn heart.

I was right, and he does look like my sister. I wonder for the briefest moment if my baby would've looked like this, too, so pink and perfect. It's only a glimmer, in which I imagine myself as a mother and realize how far away I am from that reality, all in the same breath. I realize I wouldn't have the faintest clue how to feel if this little guy was mine to care for. None of this hurts like I thought it would, though. Maybe on another day it will, but right now I'm smiling bigger than I ever have in my life, and these tears in my eyes are springing from absolute happiness. Then again, maybe tears of joy are a fallacy; that with all happiness there is also sadness.

"You did it," I say, passing him back to her. "I told you you could."

"I know I probably sounded like a crazy person."

"Twenty-four hours of physical torture will do that a person."

I crouch and take their picture. The first of hundreds. Ellie historically hates it when I do this, without giving her time to adjust her hair or check her makeup. Now, in that faded blue hospital gown, with hair whisping out of her lopsided ponytail and three-day old mascara smudged under her tired eyes, she just smiles. I want to capture every detail. The tiny bracelets, the softly beeping monitors, that quiet serenity when she closes her eyes and breathes in the smell of his fuzzy little head. His squirmy yawns, squinting stares, and those little fox-faced socks. Big album moments. I could capture a thousand stills and it would never be enough.

"I'm sorry, Ellie," I finally sigh. "About the shower. I really didn't mean to ruin it."

The corner of her mouth shrugs itself into a sort of smile. She's so willing to forgive me it hurts. I have to imagine the hormones and holiday vibes have something to do with this.

"At least it's a good story right?"

"Oh sure. 'My sister told me to eff off at my own baby shower'. Classic."

She gives a half-hearted laugh and smiles down at the swaddle in her arms. Somewhere down the hall, a phone rings and a muted conversation slides past. The faint scent of gardenia lingers from the bouquet on her bedside table. Her next words surround us just as softly.

"I just want you to be happy for me."

That guilty pang aches through my chest.

"I am. I really am. It so wasn't about you. I know that sounds like a line, but I mean it. It's just... it's been a long year."

"Nate," she nods.

"Not just Nate," I admit.

"The booze?"

"The... what? No. It's not the booze. I mean, yes, I drank too much at the shower, but that was an accident. Who knew you could get drunk off that stuff? It tasted like pie filling."

"Okay," she laughs. "Then what is it? Really."

All I can do is sigh. I want to tell her, I do. A part of me even needs to tell her, not for absolution but for the simple fact of having someone to share this truth with, so I'm not just carrying it alone. But I look at the baby in her arms, and I just can't. Not here. Not now. Not in this shiny, perfect moment.

"Another time, okay? I'm not really... I just don't think I have all the right words yet."

Uncertainty creeps across her features. I can see her puzzling through the possible scenarios of my spiraling demise, like maybe I'm struggling with an addiction or a rare disease or the fallout from some scandalous affair. I wonder, if I were in her position, which one would win out.

"Okay," she nods. "You know, you can have Mr. Snugglebottom. If you want."

"Are you just saying that to make me feel better?"

"No," she defends.

"The fact that you're not willing to fight me to the death over this is a sure sign that you are."

"I just had a baby," she laughs. "I don't think I'm in the shape to fight anyone for anything. Except maybe sleep. I could probably fight someone for that right about now."

"Fair enough. But seriously. I think he'll be a good pal for Silas. You'll have to tell him all the good stories we made up, about his pirate days --"

"Captain Snugglebottom," she nods.

"And his dragon taming days."

"Snugglebottom the Great, I think it was?"

"And his time as a British spy."

"That's Snugglebottom," she says in a James Bond accent. "Mister Snugglebottom."

"He's a bear of many talents."

We settle into the kind of smiles that don't hold back. This happiness is as quiet as the infant in her arms. I watch the subtle way he moves with her breath, and he feels like such a miracle. If only one of us got the miracle, I'm happy it was her.

When Robbie and my parents return, we all hover around that narrow bed. I steal pictures of my parents – now grandparents – with adoring smiles on their faces and their hands on each others' shoulders. Robbie squeezes onto the bed with Ellie, and I snag a shot of the three of them, as their whole life together is just beginning.

"Scrunch in," I say, motioning all of them in. "I want to get one of everybody."

"No," Ellie protests.

I wonder if now, after a million pictures, she's going to return to her former vanity, but she gives me a grin.

"It's not everybody without you. You've got to get in here, too."

I prop the camera on the counter by the sink and set the timer. My dad wraps his arm around me as I join them in the frame. We laugh through a few clicks and settle into smiles for the last snaps. I slide it back into my bag, resisting the urge to cycle through the images now, because for once I want to save them. I can already see this moment for what it is: love, and lots of it.

Before I leave, Ellie pulls me in close.

"Even if you don't find the right words," she says, "about, ya know, whatever it is -- I'm here for whichever ones you've got, whenever you're ready. Just so you know."

"Thanks, El," I say. I realize I'm blinking back tears. "When did you get so wise?"

"Lots of years trying to be just like you."

I roll my eyes because it's such clear pandering, but it pulls at my strings anyway. "Am I a shameless suck-up, too?"

She ignores this jab with another light-hearted laugh.

"I'm so glad you came. For this, obviously, but also because I just couldn't stand the thought of you spending Christmas alone."

It's a tiny flicker, like those candles in the church, but I think about Miles in his stupid sweaters and about Major Tom sleeping on top of the piano. I think about the little Christmas tree, and that single pair of stockings, and how if I was walking through this scene like Ebenezer with the Ghost of Christmas Present, I might wish I was sitting there with them, eating cinnamon sugar poptarts in that red velvet chair.

"Yeah," I say, kissing the top of her head. "Me, too."

***

I have Christmas lunch with my parents in the hospital cafeteria. Poinsettias decorate the tables, sparkly garlands line the buffet, and snowflake decals adorn the foggy windows. We eat sliced turkey with cranberry jelly and something resembling green bean casserole on trays that remind me of high school. It's not the spread my mom usually prepares, and it needs salt, but it's plenty festive. My parents regale me with stories from the past couple of days, beginning with Ellie's contractions.

"We got halfway here when we realized Julius had jumped in the car with us. You should've seen his excited little face," Mom laughs, imitating the ear-to-ear pant of my sister's beloved bulldog.

"What did you do?" I say.

"Of course we had to turn around and take him back. Robbie said Ellie was yelling at him the rest of the way there, asking if we knew which hospital it was."

I laugh, because I could totally see her doing this.

"Man, it feels like that was weeks ago at this point," my dad offers.

"Don't I know it," I say.

I fork through a piece of gooey pecan pie.

"Before you head back," my mom says, "we wanted to give you this."

She produces a plastic container from her bag. It's still slightly warm and full of French toast. I'm already overflowing with gratitude when she adds, "And this."

She places a white envelope on top. When I flip it open, I find the rest of the rent I've been scrambling to come up with. And then some. I haven't said anything, not even to Ellie, so I don't know where this is coming from. I give them a pained look.

"Really. You guys didn't have to –"

"We wanted to," Dad says.

"And we know it's been a hard year, with Nate moving out," Mom offers.

"Okay, is this about the baby shower, again? Because I –"

"Oh, Cee, do you really have to bring that up? It's Christmas," Mom says. "Can't we just do something nice for you?"

"Sure, Mom, of course. But this is a lot more than 'nice'. This is –"

"What your mother means to say," Dad interjects, "is that we know you've been doing it all on your own."

"But –"

He holds up a hand, adding, "And we know you're doing great."

"Okay, but –"

"And we know you would never ask us for anything."

I narrow my eyes at him now, because he is definitely my father. He knows I don't want my parents' money, or pity money, or even we're-giving-you-this-so-we-don't-have-to-talk-about-your-emotional-breakdown money. I glance at the envelope with a sigh.

"But that's the best part about playing Santa," Mom smiles. "Sometimes you don't have to ask. Sometimes Santa just knows."

There's a twinkle in her eye, and this moment is so sincere. It's filling up my chest until I feel like there isn't room for anything else. So naturally, this is when my dad throws in, "And I never liked that Nate guy, anyway."

My mom elbows him like he ruined the moment, but he chuckles and rubs his side.

"Thanks, Dad," I say. And I still think it's pretty perfect.

"How is Nate doing, anyway?" Mom asks.

Well, almost perfect.

"However he's doing, I'm glad he's doing it far away from me."

"Oh," she says. "Did something happen between you two?"

I want to roll my eyes, but I find myself laughing instead. "You do remember we broke up, right? I did tell you that?"

She's stammering like she's about to make some sort of excuse, until my dad says, "Honey."

Mom nods now, giving us both a begrudging smile. "Yes, I remember. He just seemed like such a –"

"Mom."

"Okay, okay. I'm sorry. Now I don't know what to say! What can I say?"

"Good riddance," I offer.

"Good riddance," she agrees.

My dad raises his plastic cup of sweet tea to us, and we all follow suit. We tip them together over the top of our almost-empty trays in a cafeteria toast. For the rest of our lives, we'll remember this Christmas for all the ways it isn't like any other, but for right now I'm grateful for all the ways it is. I've got my family, as dysfunctional as we can be. I've got love, as ridiculous as it might sound. And I've got a reason, however small, to still believe in magic.

25.

When I make it back to my apartment, it's darker than it was when I left. I see the lamps glowing through Miles's window, and I know he's home, but I don't knock. The holiday makes my shadowy windows and cheerless living room feel especially forlorn. But more than this, I notice that it's... warm. I ease out of my coat, testing the temperature. This can't be right.

I move into the hallway and confirm it with the thermostat. "Hallelujah," I say.

I don't know who they would've called it to fix it today, but I'm not complaining. I chalk it up to another Christmas miracle. I eat a piece of French toast cold, straight from the container, before crawling into bed and pulling the blankets up to my chin. I let the exhaustion settle into my limbs and want nothing more than to wake up in the morning and have this holiday behind me, as strangely wonderful as parts of it have been.

I'm not sure if I've been asleep for minutes, or hours, or at all.

The notes drift through the wall and into my twilight sleep. That same old familiar melody dances between his place and mine. I open my eyes, annoyed.

"Really?" I sigh aloud.

I wrench the blankets more tightly around me and bury my face in the pillows. I will not give him the satisfaction of storming over there. I'm thinking about pounding against the wall until he shuts up, when I hear it. That subtle shift, where the song reaches past the point that it usually ends.

I sit up to listen.

The melody fills itself out. It's tentative at first. Testing. Teasing. It takes my breath a little, the way he did when he kissed me on that rooftop and leaned into me in that snowy street. The notes build, with every run lining up like they've always been there and sweeping into something that tingles up my arms and tugs through my chest. I can almost see the way he leans into it. Closing his eyes. Dripping with feeling.

I'm still, barely breathing, like I think any little movement might ruin the moment, and I don't want it to end. It doesn't. It soars through what sounds like a chorus and winds itself into a bridge. It fits together like it's the only way it ever could have gone. When it ends, he starts again, just the same way as before.

I have no idea what I'm doing.

I throw off the blankets, run barefoot across the shared porch, and bang heavy against the paint-chipped wood. I wait with my heart in my throat and my breath coming in quick clouds against the cold. I'm already knocking again, leaning my weight into it, when the door swings open.

He's standing there in athletic pants and a crew-neck sweater that looks way too good on him. It brings out the blue in his eyes, and the way they're just blinking at me, two parts wary and one part stunned.

"I didn't know you were home," he says.

"I just got back," I offer. "You finished the song."

"Yeah, um, maybe."

He sighs, running a hand up the back of his hair. The soles of my feet are already freezing, and I shift, wondering exactly why I'm standing out here. My head is jumbled with all the things I can't figure out how to say, so I offer one at random.

"I watched *A Christmas Carol*. The one with Patrick Stewart."

He's just blinking at me, and I should probably add something more. Something like, "You were right." About it. About us. About me. Instead I just stand there, watching his gaze puzzle across my face, like he can solve all my mysteries.

"And?"

"And I think I'm in love with you."

His gaze holds mine, questioning, stunned, and I suck in another breath.

"I am," I correct. "In love with you."

There's something about those moments, when you put yourself out there, when you make yourself vulnerable, that makes them stretch. Those seconds feel long, and my limbs are tingling with terror, and my heart is racing with hope. Every other time I've ever said it in my life has been a sure thing, and I knew that those guys – with their boyfriend scripts and husband material veneers – would always say it back.

He doesn't say it back.

Instead he says, "You don't have to do this."

I bite my lip. "No, I really do. I'm tired of pretending, Miles. I've been pretending that this year hasn't ripped me apart – it did. And that I don't have feelings for you – I do. And that that doesn't scare the fuck out of me – it really, really does. But I'm scared if I don't do this now that I'm going to regret it for the rest of my life. I'm not afraid of being alone, but I'm afraid of missing this chance. With you. I never wanted to be your one-night stand."

His gaze dances across my face. He watches me for a moment like he's waiting for me to change my mind.

"Cecilia," he sighs. "Are you sure about this? Because I can't keep striking things from the record with us. I can't forget anything about you. Trust me, I've tried." He looks pained now. "And for the record, I never wanted you to be my one-night stand."

I soften. "You know you could've just told me that. With less, ya know, cursing. When we were fully dressed."

The memory brings red into his cheeks.

"And you would've believed me?"

I chew the inside of my lip, considering. Honestly? I probably would've thought he was playing me, that pulling at my strings was just one of his many mind tricks. Or maybe I would've thought this was happening too fast, that it wasn't smart to play games with a heart so recently broken. At the very least, I would've overthought it, enough that I might have second-guessed the whole thing, and put it off until tomorrow, and gone home alone.

"I dunno," I say. "You could've just gone along with it. Most guys would have."

"I'm not most guys."

"I know."

"And I didn't want you to leave feeling the way I knew you'd be feeling if you thought this was nothing," he says.

"I never thought this was nothing," I admit.

"You know you could've just told me that."

His look tightens through my chest, and that desperate feeling spreads through me. It's in the way he sighs as I bridge the space between us, the way his hands snake up to frame my face, bringing that probing gaze to meet mine.

"We should probably work on our communication skills," I say softly.

"Probably," he smiles. "But there are just so many other things to do with our mouths."

We kiss through those explanations he hasn't yet given and those questions I haven't yet asked. We are instant-combustible-keep-open-from-open-flame heat. His fingers thread through my hair. He's pulling me into the warm intensity of his kiss, and I melt into him like the fading snow.

This is everything.

We ease into his apartment. I am coursing with want and need and the inability to do anything other than lean into it. He's smoothing his hands down my waist and nipping at my neck.

"You know I'm still your neighbor, right? And I am especially averse to the suburbs. And I think families are about the most fucked up things in existence."

"I know."

"And I'm kind of crazy, hopelessly in love with you."

"Yeah?"

"Yeah."

"I don't wanna be your one-night stand, but I really wanna fuck you now," I murmur against his lips, "just so we're clear."

"God yes," he breathes.

He scoops me up and wraps me around him. I'm kissing him hard as we crash through the door, and against the desk, and we make it all the way to the bed this time. His pants are already pooling around his ankles, my shirt is already on the floor. He drops me against the soft spring of his mattress as he's tearing off my little pajama shorts and kissing his way down the swell of my breasts.

"You're so fucking good at this," I groan.

His smile tingles against my skin. "You still sound surprised."

I'm not. Not even a little. I'm reveling in the excitement that he knows exactly what he does to me. When he licks at my nipples. When he bites at my neck. When he drags his fingers down my body until they dip into the slick heat between my legs.

A shuddering sound escapes him, like he can't take how I'm already aching for him.

"Do you have any idea how much I missed you?" he breathes.

I close my eyes. I maybe mean to respond, but the only thing I can manage is a moan. He kisses down my throat and teases at my sensitive, swollen center. I hear myself moan again. I clutch into him like I can hold onto this feeling.

He is hopeless, and I am breathless, and I don't have to beg. He rips open that black foil packaging with his teeth and tugs me under him in one quick flex of muscle, like he needs me, like he owns me. He is so magnificently hard, and he's hooking the backs of my knees over his arms, one after another, the same way he laid me across that chair, until I'm spread open beneath him. I arch against the distance between us with a pleading sound. Every part of me wants him. Wants the way he is all over me, and on top of me, and sinking inside me.

My breath breaks. I grip into his arms, his shoulders, his chest. *Yes. Please. Yes.*

For a second he doesn't move, just teases at my mouth with his, like he can drink in those soft little sighs.

"God, you're fucking perfect."

He says it into my skin as he sinks into me again. And again. And nothing has ever felt this good. He watches it take me over, watches that moment I become his, wholly, unthinking. I pull my hands through his hair, bite into his bottom lip, dragging him deeper, as my want becomes need. Hot, desperate, consuming.

"Yes," I breathe. "Yes."

I need everything about the way he moves in me, with me, for me. He angles his hips harder into mine, thrusting into every sensitive spot, until he's got me just like he wants me, sexy and screaming, and I don't think anyone has ever looked at me like this, and I am pleasure, and I am agony, and I am so very close.

He knows it. He can taste it on my lips and feel it in the way my skin goes taut as he drags his hands across me. If our bodies are the rhythm, these desperate sounds are the chorus. He holds me at the edge until I'm pleading, with him, with god, with every thrust of that hard, perfect cock.

I can barely think, barely breathe.

"God. Miles. Please. Holy fuck."

Just when I think I'm going to lose my whole fucking mind from the feel of him, release crashes through me. That throbbing pulse of pleasure takes me over, tightens around him until I cease to be. I am nowhere and everywhere, now and never. He's made me come before, but never like this. I know he can feel it. I feel the way he slows, the gentle way he kisses me again, the way he holds me like I might break. I close my eyes to catch my breath, but I don't let him go.

"Do you want me to stop?" he asks.

"Is that a joke?" I breathe.

He brings that smile to my neck. When he moves again he's deep and deliberate and my sighs are a hopeless sound because I can't understand how anything has ever felt this good. He's not holding back anymore. He drags me even closer, wrapping a leg around his torso, kissing my wrists as my fingers wind themselves into his hair. I'm already trembling at the edge again, moaning prayers into his mouth.

"Fuck, Cecilia," he breathes. "*Fuck*."

We are desire and desperation. We are too fucking close. I can tell he's fighting it. He slows with a ragged breath, just long enough for me to reverse our positions. He groans as I slide all the way against him. I love that sound he makes, love being on top of him, love the way he looks at me like he's about to lose it.

His fingers dig into my hips. "If you don't... slow down..."

It's been four days of foreplay: there's no way I'm slowing down. I need him, need this. My breath comes hard and desperate.

"Please don't make me stop," I say.

He growls in response, like he can't believe he's got me right here, on top of him, begging him. He's dragging me against him, until I'm moaning into his mouth and he's biting kisses down my neck, until we're so, fucking, close.

I feel him tense, hear the break in his breath, see that momentary flash of desperation in his eyes. His release throbs through me. That feeling is all it takes to push me over the edge again. Those waves of pleasure crash through me, until I'm not sure if it's him or me that's still coming, until we're kissing through the wake, until we're nothing but skin and breath and heat.

He pulls me into his arms, running his fingers up the back of my neck. My entire body shudders in satisfaction. I melt into him.

"I love you," he says, grazing the words against me. "I'm in love with you, too."

***

We share wine and French toast in the middle of his living room floor, dressed enough to seem decent, while Major Tom rolls across the rug with his new catnip toy. I can hear him purring from where we sit. When I smile, my lips feel swollen from all the kisses. I sink back against the red velvet chair.

"You never told me what it meant," I say. "The devils and the details."

He smiles. "It's not all that clever."

"Tell me anyway."

"It's something my grandfather used to say a lot. He said the actual phrase, of course, but when I was a kid I always heard it like that. The devils and the details. I felt like it made sense, though. I thought the devils were all the hard, shitty things in your life. The things that give you hell."

"You thought this... as a kid?"

"You met my mom," he says. "I had a lot of devils, though. Not all of them her fault. And I fought them for a long time."

"Like what?"

"Life. Death. The way that the space between those two things is challenging, and complicated, and... inexplicably short."

I nod, understanding. This thought seems too heavy, and he pulls himself up and pours a little more wine, before sliding in front of that piano. His hands fall across the keys easily, slipping into that melody that lured me over here. I slide in beside him.

"And the details?"

"The details are the things that distinguish anything from everything."

"I don't get it."

"Yeah you do," he smiles. "You're one of those people who actually does get it. You notice things. The little things. I knew it that first day I saw you. First day – not first night. You stood outside for almost thirty minutes taking pictures of the walkway out front."

"It's a great walkway," I defend. "There are names and handprints in it from the sixties."

"Yes, but nobody cares about things like that. At least not enough to stand out there taking pictures. For half an hour. But you did. And I noticed."

It shivers up my spine.

"Why?"

"Because the details matter. They always have, maybe more than the devils, because they show you how things can be different. Sometimes that's what gets you through, you know? Knowing that no matter how bad things get, things can be different. Like today from yesterday. And you from every other girl. And this song from all the ones I ever wrote."

I smile as his fingers dance across the keys.

"Did you start playing this just so I would come over?"

"No," he laughs. "I actually didn't think you were ever going to come over here again."

"Seriously?"

He shrugs. "Last time we only flirted, and I barely talked to you for three years."

I roll my eyes, laughing in spite of myself.

"So you were just going to go back to being my enemy?"

"What? I was never your enemy," he scoffs.

I give him a look.

"I fixed your furnace!" he defends.

"What? When? Why?" Then, "How?"

"When you were gone, I guess. It's up in the attic. Just because we didn't have sex didn't mean I wanted you to freeze to death over there."

"Okay, but *how*?"

"There's an automatic shutoff when it can't get enough air. I just reset it. When's the last time you changed that filter?"

"Um, never?"

"Well, there's your problem."

"Well, good thing now I've got you."

He kisses me, and that impossible feeling surges through me again. I know it's not just him, necessarily, but us. Maybe it's science, or chemistry, as inevitable as cold fronts and weather patterns. Whatever it is, I never want it to end. I want to recreate it everyday, over and over again.

"This is my favorite Christmas tradition," he admits.

"Oh yeah? Which part? So far we've got... French toast, snowball fights, church, a crazy ex, a minor emotional breakdown, Patrick Stewart, the merengue, and really great make-up sex. Does that about cover it?"

"You forgot the part where I made you come on the couch."

"I definitely didn't forget that part," I smile.

"And in the shower."

"That one either," I laugh.

"You," he breathes. "To answer your original question. Just you. Too cliché?"

"Yes," I offer between kisses. "But I love it."

As those last hours of Christmas are slipping towards the next day, I'm climbing onto his lap, and he's pulling me against him. The fire is familiar, but this one's a slow burn. I'm kissing him on the bench, and making him moan while I'm on my knees, and losing my breath as we tangle ourselves against the rug. That heat spreads under our skin until it's too hot to keep our clothes on and licks through us until it hurts too much to stay apart. We've spent days grasping at these moments like we're worried they won't last, but this one lingers like his gaze on my body and me against his chest after everything in us is spent.

As we lie beside the little tree, his fingers are gently threading into my hair, and I am listening to the way his heart is pounding like the heat in my veins and the echoes of pleasure in my bones.

"What are we doing?" I whisper.

His words vibrate against me. "What do you wanna do?"

"I don't really have a plan."

"That's a first," he laughs. "How about dinner, tomorrow?"

"Dinner," I smile. "That's your idea of a plan?"

"Only if you say yes."

I trace my fingers down his chest, feeling the way his breath has gone quiet. The moment stretches with vulnerability and stills with hope. The string lights glow across our skin, bathing us in late-night magic. I breathe through this feeling, like I've never felt so content to be anywhere, and I've never been so excited about finding out everywhere this moment might lead. If this is love, we've made it. I won't even use air quotes this time.

"Yes."

26.

I TAKE OFF MY COAT AS I STEP INTO MATILDA'S, wondering why I even bothered with it tonight, and ease through the crowd. They're already restless. Maybe it's a signature of mid-winter spring, when your calendar says December but you've got your windows open and feel like this would be a good time to clean out your closets, or go wash your car, or maybe fall in love. The guys have got the sleeves of their sweaters rolled up, and the girls are wearing those sparkly smiles that they're hoping might snag a guy who will stick around until actual spring. As much as I'm a sucker for finding someone to spend hibernation season with, that's not on tonight's agenda.

When I get to the bar, Ari spots me immediately -- per her regulars radar -- and brings me a cocktail. I should maybe be a little concerned that the bartender knows both me and my drink, but I smile and slide onto the only open barstool in the corner.

"I didn't know if I'd see you tonight."

"The party ended early," I shrug. "Mr. Moretti caught Mrs. Moretti making out with his son, recently home from college, under the mistletoe. Let's just say the rum punch was not the only punch served at the event. One bloody nose, a few broken fingers, and two very drunk secretaries live-streaming the entire thing. The pictures were pretty much over after that."

"Yup," Ari laughs. "That'll do it."

I take a sip of my cocktail, and it's everything I need it to be: fizzy, citrusy, and strong. The bar is full tonight, and I spot Cat Glasses and Fabulous Fedora across the way, giving me a wave and a tip of the hat, respectively. That booth against the wall is sitting full of a foursome I don't recognize, and I'm still smiling about the fact that somebody drew a very large penis over the spot where my name used to be. Now it just says Nate + dick. I'll give you two guesses who the artist was, but I bet you only need one.

I barely hear the door chime over the din of conversation, but I don't miss the grimace on Ari's face.

"Oh god. Who brings a baby to a bar?"

I follow her gaze to see Eleanor and Robbie wandering in. They look a little out of place, like maybe they thought this was not a bar but a Banana Republic. My brother-in-law looks especially bewildered about the seating arrangements, but my sister seems determined to make this work. Silas is strapped to her chest, wearing ginormous, noise-cancelling headphones.

"My sister," I reply, scrunching up my nose.

"Should've known," she laughs. "They drinking?"

"I hope so," I say.

I wave them down with an incredulous grin and pull them into a hug.

"I thought you weren't coming until Christmas!"

"Plans change," Ellie shrugs. "I'm trying to be more like you, ya know? Young and spontaneous."

"That is so not you. Or me. But I've got a room for you all made up! Ah, I'm so glad you're here!"

I kiss baby Silas, who is now more of an almost-toddler, on the head.

"Happy birthday, bud," I say, though I know he can't hear me. To Ellie and Robbie I add, "You wanna grab a table?"

"Sure!" they say in unison, but they're already exchanging a nervous look like they don't understand where I'm going to find such a thing.

"C'mon. I know a guy."

There's only one abandoned up front, and it is stacked with a guitar case, an extra set of drumsticks, and two cans of Red Bull. I quickly clear it and drag it into commission. We settle in, and Ari brings us a round of drinks: a beer for Robbie, plum wine for Eleanor, and an Old Fashioned for the corner of the piano. Miles winks at me as he takes a sip, and my heart flips like it always does.

"You're here early," he mouths.

I give him a smile and a shrug. "Maybe I missed you."

He's giving me one of those looks and sweeping a hand through his hair. His eyes are bright with anticipation, and this electric feeling is one of my favorites, that buzz just before a show begins.

"How y'all doing this evening?" he asks into the mic.

The crowd around us cheers, and he smiles.

"What's everybody drinking tonight?"

The cheers turn into whistles and whoops, and I can't help but laugh, because he's too good at this. He brings his hands to the keys. The mood is festive, and despite the fact it was almost seventy degrees today in the sun, plenty of spectators are adorned with jingle bell earrings, and red-and-green outfits, and blinking headbands, as if we won't all be wearing flip flops and having drinks on the patio by Christmas. I think I see Dancing

Santa jiving through the mix, though he's not wearing a Santa hat this year, and Holly Danford isn't calling for snow. As such, when Joss arrives, she's wearing a slinky tank top and sandals. Dancing Santa eyes her up and down as she makes her way to our table, just as those first notes start.

"He's cute," she offers, glancing over her shoulder.

"Almost married with a kid," I warn.

"God, aren't they all."

She, Ellie, and Robbie exchange season's greetings amid Miles's opening banter, and Joss drags Silas into her lap in an instant.

"Oh, now, *you're* cute," she says to him. "Check out those eyes."

"That's how he gets you," Eleanor says. "He looks all innocent and sweet, then he pukes on you and doesn't let you sleep for days."

"Sounds like my last boyfriend," Joss snorts.

"Well, that's why he's got a Cee-Cee and an Auntie Joss," I say. "To remind him he's one of the good ones."

She giggles, repeating this back to him, and her voice is a coo, though he can't hear her.

The opening notes to "All I Want for Christmas" are tinkling through the bar, and I smile as the anticipation builds, because I know what comes next. The first line of the verse crashes through the space. People are singing along, and screaming along, and Dancing Santa is living up to his namesake and rocking through the crowd. Everything is electric, and I feel it, too, even though I hear this all the time now. I come home to it, and wake up to it, and sometimes even fall asleep to it. As annoying as it used to be coming from his place, now that it's filling up our place, it's kind of my favorite thing.

After months of only going to my apartment for clothes, when he got back from his last leg of the summer tour we made the move official. I met him on the porch and leapt into his arms, and we tumbled down the stairs even though there wasn't any snow. He wrapped my legs around him as we rolled in the grass and laughed. He kissed me once, and twice, and a hundred times over, like he couldn't get enough.

"You're never allowed to leave again," I said.

He smoothed his hands through my hair, breathing in my smell and tasting my lips.

"I never want to leave again."

I added my lamps to his living room, my art to his walls, and my books to his shelves. I was always at his place anyway. I took care of Major Tom when he was on the road, and organized all his records, and framed that picture from the stayed-up-all-night snowy morning to sit on his piano. I still had space in the corner of the spare room for that home office. Because, ya know, boundaries.

The guy who moved into my old place is named Harmon. He is a curly-headed college senior who smokes way too much weed, throws way too many parties, and plays his music after midnight. We hope, maybe, that he'll grow out of all those things that make him so annoying. Or move. In the meantime, we've got our own ways to make too much noise after midnight, all of which I find infinitely more entertaining than Harmon's acid house electronica.

The rounds of drinks disappear, and Ellie is laughing until her curls fall in her face, and Robbie is smiling as he sweeps them behind her ear. All I want for Christmas is this: all of my favorite people, right here, in one place. I don't need snow, or carols, or boxes wrapped with string. I just need this warm glow, and this happy feeling, and the knowledge that when I get home we'll have a full apartment and a festive little tree.

"Before we break, I just want to take a moment to make a Christmas wish come true," Miles says, leaning into those chords I've come to know so well. If we have a song, this is it. I smile, glancing over my shoulder, wondering which couple asked him to play it.

"Because somebody," he continues, "is either about to have the best night of his life or make a complete fucking fool of himself."

A few stray cheers whoop up from the crowd, and I smile, because I love when people do this. When you see that nervous guy walk up to the band, and he's so in love he doesn't care how cliche it seems when he tells them he's going to propose. That's love, I think. Not a sprint, but a marathon. Something that requires endurance, and a willingness to take something way further than anyone with good sense would. It makes me wish I had my camera, just to capture the looks on their faces, just to give them one for the album.

His hands move effortlessly through the opening lines, but he's not singing the lyrics that now accompany them, and he doesn't call anybody up to the stage. I deflate a little, realizing maybe this isn't a proposal. Actually I don't know what this is. But I know it starts with, "Some of you know my girlfriend Cecilia."

I stop looking around now and meet his gaze. My heart skips a beat.

"And maybe some of you know that before she became my girlfriend, I spent a few years as her asshole neighbor."

The crowd laughs on cue.

"No, seriously. That's actually what she called me: 'my asshole neighbor'. I had my own acronym," he laughs. "I'm not gonna say I didn't deserve it."

Joss is giving me an amused sidelong glance now, and I meet it with a mute smile and a shake of my head, because even though it's hilariously true, I have no idea where he's going with this.

"But last Christmas, two crazy things happened. One: she fell in love with me. And two: it fucking snowed. And if you had asked me which one of those things I thought was the least likely to happen, I wouldn't have gone with the snow."

Even I'm laughing now, though my eyes are blurring with tears, and where exactly *is* he going with this? I take a sip of my cocktail and try to keep my cool, because I'm too hopeful about what this is and too terrified of being wrong. But the way he's looking at me is everything, and Ellie is intermittently smiling at me, and now Joss won't even look my way. And no, I think. No, no, no. We haven't really talked about this. I haven't even mentioned it, because even though I know how he feels about me, I also know how he feels about weddings, and marriage, and settling down. Nothing about the way he loves me is settled. It's an easily excitable simmer, always tingling under the surface, ready to leave us gasping for air when it drags us under. It's all those perfect, everyday details. The way he kisses me still like he can't get enough. In my mind, we could be together for a hundred years and never even get to this.

"So I wrote her this song, because I don't know how to build a house with my bare hands like that guy in *The Notebook*. And I'm actually way ahead of schedule here, because it didn't take me seven years to finish it. And -- man, I'm really bad at this," he laughs, shaking his head. He takes a swig of his drink, and finally, his gaze finds mine again.

"Cecilia, I know for a long time I was just that guy next door who drove you crazy, and I know that sometimes we still drive each other crazy, and I know we're all gonna die in the end. But can we just... keep driving each other crazy every day until then?"

I suck in a breath, and I can feel every pair of eyes at my table on me. That's why they're here, I realize. This is why Eleanor and Robbie came in early. Why Joss rearranged her usual travel plans. I'm always the planner, and yet, he planned this. He switches to that one-hand melody and pulls a box out of his pocket, and I know without opening it that it's not a heart-shaped necklace. My eyes spring with tears.

The bar is buzzing with questions, but the only one I need to hear is right there on his lips.

"I guess what I mean to say is, will you marry me?"

I never break his gaze, but the tears slide down my face anyway. I roll my eyes, because he knew that I would cry, and I don't even care that it's happening in front of all these people, because I love him. There's no photographer waiting in the wings, no one to record this big album moment, but I love him. He's kind, and yet still kind of an asshole, and I love him. Always. Always always. Two times infinity.

I glance at Joss, and she shrugs.

"When you know you know, boo."

And I don't know how he knew. I never told him I wanted all my friends here, never said I wanted the opal ring that's waiting in that box. And I think maybe this is the best thing about Christmas: sometimes you don't have to ask. Sometimes Santa just knows.

I down the rest of my drink, pull myself out of my chair, and a few people wolf whistle as I slide onto the bench beside him. He's still playing with one hand as he grabs the box and flips it open. I'm still giving him a look as he places it perfectly on my finger.

"Yes," I say.

"Yes?" he says. "You're not just saying that because of all these people?"

"Just kiss me, you jerk."

The notes falter as my mouth meets his, and eventually stop altogether, giving way to his hands framing my face, and the applause rising around us. The cymbals simmer and crash, like this moment has its own climactic sizzle, and I break us apart with a laugh. He brushes tears from my cheeks with the back of his hand, and the entire year stretches out behind us, and for once my mind doesn't skip ahead. I don't know what day of the week it'll be, or what kind of dress I'll wear, or what type of wine we'll drink. I'm right here, held tight in this moment, and I don't even know where to begin, so I kiss him again.

About the Author

Heather McPeake is a full-time corporate professional, part-time yoga instructor, and lifelong late-night writer. She lives with her husband and their houseful of pets in Memphis, TN. Sometimes it actually snows.

For updates, follow her on Instagram: @heathermcwrites